They sat on the sofa and Madison immediately felt comfortable with Stuart. He was quite handsome and seemed interested in her. How could she not feel the same way?

"What are you thinking?" Stuart peered into her eyes as he tried to process his good fortune of being in the company of a gorgeous woman.

"That I'd love to kiss you," she said. *Had she really just said that to him? Where did the courage come from?*

"Then do it," he told her, taking her wineglass and setting it on the coffee table beside his. "Or, better yet, let me kiss you...."

Stuart tilted his face and moved in to her waiting lips parted slightly as he kissed her. Her lips were soft and tender, just as he liked them. He wrapped his arms around the small of her back and drew her even closer while continuing the kiss.

Madison caught her breath as her lips locked with Stuart's in a full-blown, openmouthed kiss. She couldn't remember ever feeling this kind of emotion from a kiss.

Books by Devon Vaughn Archer

Harlequin Kimani Romance

Christmas Heat
Destined to Meet
Kissing the Man Next Door
Christmas Diamonds
Pleasure in Hawaii
Private Luau
Aloha Fantasy
Love is in the Air
Say it with Roses

DEVON VAUGHN ARCHER

is the bestselling author of several Harlequin Kimani Romance novels, including *Love is in the Air*. He also penned *Pleasure In Hawaii*, *Private Luau* and *Aloha Fantasy*, a series which takes place on different Hawaiian islands; and holiday classics, such as *Christmas Diamonds* and *Christmas Wishes*. Archer was the first male author to write for Harlequin's Arabesque line with the tender love story, *Love Once Again*.

The author has also written a number of bestselling urban and mainstream fiction, including *Danger At Every Turn*, *The Hitman's Woman* and *The Secrets of Paradise Bay*; as well as hot-selling young-adult fiction, such as the *Her Teen Dream* and *His Teen Dream* series.

To keep up with his latest news and upcoming books, follow, friend or connect with Devon Vaughn Archer on Twitter, Facebook, YouTube, LinkedIn, MySpace, Goodreads, LibraryThing and www.devonvaughnarcher.com.

SAY IT WITH

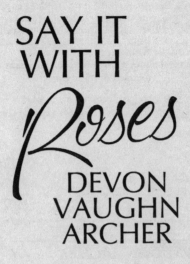

Roses

DEVON VAUGHN ARCHER

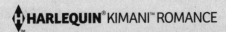

HARLEQUIN® KIMANI™ ROMANCE

To H. Loraine, the love of my own life who keeps me on my
toes and down to earth.

And to my fans who have inspired me to keep writing great
love stories for you to enjoy for years to come.

Recycling programs
for this product may
not exist in your area.

ISBN-13: 978-0-373-86300-6

SAY IT WITH ROSES

Copyright © by R. Barri Flowers

For questions and comments about the quality of this book, please contact us
at CustomerService@Harlequin.com.

Printed in U.S.A.

Dear Reader,

I am delighted to present to you my latest heartwarming Harlequin Kimani romance. As the follow-up to the successful *Love is in the Air*, I'm sure you will feel compelled to keep turning the pages as this wonderful love story unfolds.

Sparks fly when a book reviewer moves to Portland, Oregon, and meets a handsome author and father of two adorable little girls. Both the heroine and hero have been burned in past relationships, which means they have to learn to trust each other as things heat up between them.

I believe that love the second time around is even better. This tale will make a believer out of you, too!

I invite you, as well, to read my recent Hawaii-themed romances *Aloha Fantasy, Private Luau,* and *Pleasure in Hawaii.*

Kind regards,

Devon Vaughn Archer

I would like to thank my wife, H. Loraine, for her untiring devotion to me and my writings. I owe much of my success to her and never fail to express my gratitude.

I also extend appreciation to the Harlequin Kimani editors and staff I have worked with over the years for their professionalism and support in helping to bring my romances to life.

Chapter 1

Madison Wagner could hardly believe that she was living in Portland, Oregon. Yet here she was, for two weeks now, occupying a very nice town house in a parklike setting that overlooked the Willamette River with a lovely view of Mount Hood. The place had all the modern amenities and an open floor plan, and it fit her rustic furnishings perfectly. After relocating from Houston, Texas, she had taken a job as a senior book reviewer and columnist for an upscale magazine called *Rose Petals* that was a play on the city's nickname of the Rose City. Though part of her would always consider Houston home, the better part of Madison was delighted to have a chance for a fresh start at age thirty. After being stung by an ex who basically left her at the altar three years ago, she definitely wanted out of Texas. She hoped to someday find that perfect man but would definitely proceed very carefully down that road.

It was a Saturday morning in early December, and Madison put on her helmet and got on her bicycle for some exercise. It seemed as though practically everyone in town rode their bicycles to stay fit and cut down on the costs of driving.

No sooner had Madison started up a hill surrounded by Douglas firs when she heard her name being called. She looked over her shoulder and saw Stuart Kendall. He was a big-time author who also happened to be the brother of her onetime friend Holly, now engaged to Madison's ex-fiancé. Madison had been devastated when she'd found out that Holly had started dating her ex-fiancé, and the two hadn't been close since.

The situation made things awkward between her and Stuart, to say the least. Of course, he was loyal to his sister, as he should be. But she still didn't feel it was a good idea to get too friendly with Stuart, even if he was one of the few people she knew in town. She had video-chatted with him once when things were tight between her and Holly, and he had also phoned when she first arrived in Portland, in what she assumed was just a courtesy call. The call had lasted all of two minutes; she could hear his two kids in the background and decided she should cut it short.

Stuart was on his bicycle and barreling toward her at breakneck speed as she continued up the hill. For a moment, she actually thought he might run into her, but then he slowed down.

"I thought that was you," he said. A crooked smile played on his handsome walnut-colored face. He was wearing a helmet and colorful bicycling attire.

"Yes, it's me," she said tersely, taking a breath.

"So you obviously live around here then," he said.

She nodded. "I guess you do, too."

"Yeah, just a few blocks away," he said, pointing his sable eyes toward some luxurious old homes.

"I'm just down the hill," she told him.

Stuart Kendall glanced at the row of new town-homes, guessing she lived in one of them. His sister Holly had told him that her ex-friend was relocating to Portland. Given the delicate situation between her and Madison, he thought the move was probably a good idea.

He gave Madison a quick appraisal. She was hot, even if the chilly-weather clothing kept him from getting a good look at her body. He liked her butterscotch-colored complexion, soft brown eyes and long curly hair beneath the helmet. Yes, she had a beauty that would get any man to look twice.

Madison kept riding and he stayed with her. "So have you been riding long?" he asked. "Or did you take up the sport to fit in with our lifestyle?"

She rolled her eyes at him. "I think people across the country enjoy riding bikes just as much as Oregonians," she said stiffly. "And, yes, I have been riding for most of my life."

He cocked a brow. "That's good to hear." Was it just him or was she giving him the cold shoulder? "I ride with my daughters whenever I can," he told her. "If you need someone to partner with sometime, just let me know...."

"I will," she said, then quickly added, "but I prefer to ride by myself and take the time to think about my day."

"No problem," Stuart said in a measured tone. Actually there was a problem, but not on his end. Still, he had to respect the lady's wishes to be left alone, even if he was merely trying to be hospitable to a new resident. "Guess I'll see you around then."

She forced a smile. "Sure, see you later."

Madison watched him veer off in the opposite direction. She hoped he didn't take her unfriendliness personally. It was just the way it had to be. At least till she had time to gain her bearings in Portland and put more distance between her and the past.

She continued pedaling, feeling weariness in her legs but determined to keep going.

Stuart caught up with his best friend and successful musician, Chad Schmidt. The two frequently went cycling and shot hoops together. They met the same year Stuart's wife left him. Chad, who had lost his wife to cancer a few years earlier, was someone Stuart had been able to lean on in his time of need.

"What's up, man?" Chad asked, sitting on his bike. His brown Rastafarian locks bounced atop his broad shoulders.

"I'm good," Stuart said as they tapped knuckles.

"So who was that chick I saw you talking to?"

"Just someone who wants to be left alone."

Chad chuckled. "Man, you must be losing your touch."

"I lost that when Fawn left me," Stuart grumbled.

"I doubt it," Chad said. "Just because you're choosing to lay low on the dating scene right now doesn't mean the ladies wouldn't line up in droves to go out with you. And not only because you're a great writer, though that doesn't hurt."

"I'll leave the ladies to other available men like you, for now," Stuart told him. He gazed off in the distance and watched as Madison pedaled up a hill.

"Sounds like a good plan to me," Chad said, grinning.

"Let's ride," Stuart said.

Later, he arrived at the Victorian home he shared with his seven-year-old twin daughters, Carrie and Dottie. The house was more than one hundred years old, but it had been updated with all the modern features of the twenty-first century, including granite countertops, cork and vinyl flooring, new plumbing and energy-efficient windows. The house had once been shared with Fawn, the girls' mother and Stuart's former wife, before she inexplicably bolted from their lives four years ago, leaving him alone to raise the twins.

It was a challenge Stuart, now age thirty-three, had readily accepted for the love of his girls. It had also left a wound in his heart that wasn't so easy to heal. He had to do what was best for his twins, and that meant he couldn't invite another woman into his life. The last thing he wanted was for them to get comfortable with someone who wasn't their mother, only to be disappointed if she too suddenly left.

The moment he stepped inside the huge foyer, Stuart was surrounded by Dottie and Carrie.

"Hi, Daddy," they spoke in unison. They were light-complexioned, thin and had thick black hair, currently in braids.

"Good morning, my little angels." He lifted them up one at a time and gave them each a big kiss on the cheek. Honestly, even with the subtle differences between the two, it was still hard sometimes to tell them apart. "Did you have breakfast yet?"

"No, we waited for you," Dottie said.

"Yeah, Grace said we should," Carrie added, tugging on his leg.

"Did she now?" Stuart smiled as Grace Brennan, their part-time nanny, entered the room. The twenty-one-year-old graduate student did a good job caring for the girls when he needed to do other things. Moreover, Dottie and Carrie got along with her, unlike the previous nannies he had employed.

"Good morning, Stuart," Grace said. "How was your ride?"

"It was a great workout," he answered. He loved the

way riding raised his heart rate and strengthened his legs. He thought about how Madison Wagner and her decidedly less-than-warm attitude had put a damper on his bright morning. If she acted like that before she even got to know him, he could only imagine how she might treat his kids if they ever ran into each other. "Why don't we all go wash up and have some breakfast," he told the girls, and added for Grace, "You're welcome to stay and eat, too." He said the polite thing, but secretly hoped she would decline as he enjoyed when it was just the three of them bonding as a family.

"I'd love to," Grace said, "but I have a hiking date with my boyfriend, so…"

"Understood," Stuart said with a smile. "Have a good hike and we'll see you the next time."

"Sounds good." Grace grabbed her bag and beamed at the girls. "Don't give your dad a hard time."

"We won't," Carrie promised, then turned to her sister. "Will we?"

"No, we won't," Dottie said. "Race you to the bathroom."

"Okay." Carrie sprinted away, giggling, with Dottie hot on her tail.

Stuart laughed, as did Grace. It gave him such joy to see them acting like girls should, rather than the way it was when their mother left and it seemed like there was a void he could never fill. While he considered it still a work-in-progress, Stuart felt he was generally getting the job done as a single parent.

* * *

On Monday, Madison drove her Subaru Legacy to the downtown offices of *Rose Petals* magazine. She loved the job, as she loved reading books and giving honest reviews. It was also nice to have her own column, where she could highlight books of interest and other general literary topics.

Stuart Kendall crossed her mind. She had not seen him since their run-in. She had read some of his thriller fiction after Holly had recommended she try it. Admittedly, he was talented, and she had given him high marks when doing reviews in Houston. But she saw little reason for them to crisscross at this point, as it would only remind her of things she was trying to forget.

After pulling into the underground parking garage, Madison took the elevator up to the fifth floor. She greeted the other members of the staff, then sat at her desk in her small office.

The editor-in-chief, Giselle Fortune, walked in holding a stack of books.

"Good morning, Madison," she said. "I've got some reading material for you."

"Oh, great!" Madison smiled as Giselle set them on her desk. "I can't wait to get started." She picked up the top book in the stack, which was a thriller by Stuart Kendall titled *The Next One to Fall*. "Hmm…this looks interesting, but I know Stuart, kind of. I used to hang out with his sister. I'd feel kind of funny reviewing his book, especially if it wasn't glowing." *Maybe even weirder if it was,* she mused.

"Understood," Giselle said. She brushed aside feathered blond hair and took the book from Madison's hands. "I'll get Larry Wellington to review it."

"Thanks," Madison said, grabbing another hardcover title that was more agreeable to her.

"I'm sure you probably already realize that Stuart's a local," Giselle said.

"Yes, my friend mentioned it to me."

"Well, just so you know," Giselle began, "while I wouldn't go so far as to say that we treat our city's best-selling authors like royalty, we do try to do pieces on them every now and then to boost circulation and show our appreciation for local talent."

And I'm sure it all goes to their heads, Madison thought. "Makes sense," she said evenly.

"That doesn't mean anyone gets a free pass for a lousy book," Giselle made clear. "As for Stuart, I met him once at a Portland book convention. He seems like a stand-up guy and totally down-to-earth."

"I'm glad to hear he's approachable," Madison told her, though she had already gathered as much. *I'd just rather not be the one to approach him right now,* she thought.

"Well, I'd better let you get to work," Giselle said. "Oh, in case I forgot to mention it, we're glad to have you as part of our team."

Madison smiled. "Thank you. I'm happy to be part of the team."

After her boss left, Madison leaned back in her chair and thought about how she could make the most of her new city and circumstances. She deserved to be happy just like everyone else. Didn't she?

Two weeks later, Madison was at home enjoying a glass of white wine and reading a book when her iPad chimed. Her sister Bianca was initiating a video chat.

Madison accepted and watched as her older sister's face suddenly appeared on the screen. "Hey there."

"Hey back at you," Bianca said. "What's going on?"

"Same old, same old," Madison responded, thinking of how much they looked alike, aside from the fact that Bianca had now gone totally blonde and had thinner brows. "Just trying to keep up with my workload."

"I hear you," Bianca said. "There's been a lot of newsworthy stuff happening at the casinos. I've had to put in extra hours at the paper." She sipped from a glass of wine. "I wish you had moved here instead of Portland. I'd love to have my kid sister around to hang out with."

"I doubt that," Madison said, smiling. Though things were good between them now, it hadn't always been that way. They were both stubborn and seemed more interested in butting into each other's lives than not. "I'd never be able to keep up with you. Besides, I like Portland and the job that brought me here."

"Fair enough. I'm sure there are some hot men in Portland to take your mind off you-know-who."

"It's already off him," Madison insisted. "That's over and done with. As for hot men in Portland, I wouldn't know, as I've been too busy to notice."

"Didn't you say Holly's brother lives there?" Bianca probed.

Damn, she has too good a memory, thought Madison, tasting her wine. "Yes, he lives here."

"And…?"

"And nothing," Madison said. "We've run into each other, but that's about it."

"He's single, right?"

"Yes, as I understand it, and he has two young children."

"Hey, there's nothing wrong with a ready-made family, if the man is a good fit," Bianca told her.

"Never said there was," Madison responded tightly. "And the man's not a good fit."

"Why not?" Bianca pressed. "Not hot enough for you?"

"He's nice-looking," she admitted. "But—"

"But he's Holly's brother and she's involved with your ex. Am I right?"

Madison saw no reason to deny it. She sighed. "Let's just say that's not a road I care to go down. And, for that matter, I'm not really interested in pursuing anyone or being pursued by anyone right now."

"Okay, okay, I won't push it," Bianca said, leaning back in her chair. "When you're ready, you can put yourself back out there. Just remember that one mistake does not a lifetime make. I've made a few mistakes in the male department, but I refuse to allow that to keep me from taking new chances at love and happiness."

"I'll try to remember that." Madison had always

prided herself on trying to keep an open mind. But, for now, she preferred to put that on the back burner and focus on work and staying active. Whatever the future brought her way, she would deal with it then.

Chapter 2

Stuart took the girls to the Oregon Zoo, knowing how much they loved seeing and hearing the animals, as he had as a kid. While part of him wished they had a mother figure to accompany them, he was just happy to be there for them himself.

After they had seen polar bears, elephants and cougars, with the girls even taking digital pictures of their favorite animals, Carrie blurted out, "Can we go on the train ride now, Daddy?"

"Yeah, let's," Dottie said.

"Two against one," Stuart said, chuckling. "You win. Let's go for a ride on the Washington Park and Zoo Railway. It'll be fun."

Ten minutes later, they were on the recreational railroad aboard a diesel-powered train that took a one-mile loop around the zoo. Stuart took delight as the girls giggled at the various sights and sounds they passed.

Before long, the ride was over, and they all got off the train. "Next time, we'll come in the summer and take the train that runs from the zoo through Washington Park," he promised, knowing they would enjoy the ride through the park forests to another station where they could disembark and visit the Rose Garden, Portland Japanese Garden and children's park.

"Promise?" Dottie asked.

"I promise," Stuart said. "Now let's head over to the Cascade Grill and get something to eat."

The girls smiled in agreement.

They enjoyed chili dogs and chips before going to see monkeys, zebras and black rhinos.

At one point, Stuart thought he spotted Madison Wagner. Was it his imagination? He thought he saw her by one of the exhibits, but she left before he could be sure it was her.

Maybe that was a good thing. He didn't want to make her uncomfortable. Or try to explain to the girls that she was once their Aunt Holly's friend till things changed.

On a Saturday afternoon in early February, Madison sat at the coffee shop reading a book she would review. She was halfway through it and found the book was only so-so.

She hadn't seen Stuart on his bike of late and imagined he had been busy between writing and raising two young children.

She flipped another page of her book and then heard a deep and resonate voice say, "Must be a pretty good book you've got there."

Looking up, Madison saw Stuart standing there, holding a paper coffee cup. "Not really," she told him. "I'm reading it for work."

He peered at her. "Aah, yes, I think Holly mentioned something about your being a book reviewer."

Madison wondered just how much Holly had told her brother about her. She was sure he knew all the ins and outs of her disaster with her former beau, which made this conversation all the more uncomfortable. "I'm working for *Rose Petals*."

Stuart nodded. "Good magazine." They had been fairly kind to him with some great reviews, including a five-star review for his latest book.

"It pays the bills," she said succinctly, hoping he would leave it at that.

Stuart was never much at small talk, especially with someone who didn't seem all that interested in speaking with him. But he couldn't stop himself from wanting to reach out to the attractive woman. Seeing her in this casual setting, without the bike helmet that had covered a good part of that gorgeous hair, made her even more appealing to him. He wondered how her ex could have let her get away.

Stuart also wondered how the same man had been smart enough to woo his sister. By all accounts, they were madly in love and planning a Valentine's Day wedding. He doubted Madison was on the invitation list.

"So how have you been doing now that you've settled in?" Stuart tossed out, sipping his coffee.

Madison had zeroed in on Stuart before he asked the question. She couldn't help but be attracted to him. He seemed to be all muscle and about six-three. His features were classically masculine and she liked his closely cropped, curly black hair.

But…she still felt it was better to steer clear of him right now, all things considered. "Look…" she began deliberately. "I'm sure you're just trying to be friendly, but I'm actually rushing to make a deadline right now."

Stuart's brow furrowed. Suddenly it had gotten frostier in the coffee shop than it was outside. "Got it. Then I'll leave you to it."

Madison offered him a strained smile and turned back to the book. But she noticed that Stuart was still standing there, prompting her to look up. "Is there something else?"

"Actually, there is," he said. "I know all about the situation with your ex and Holly. But that's between you and them, not me."

"I never said it was about you," she responded, blinking in surprise but attempting to downplay it. "That's over and done with."

"I'm not so sure about that," Stuart said honestly. "Seems to me you still have a chip on your shoulder, and you're somehow taking it out on me by association."

"That's crazy!" Madison refused to admit he was right. At least not while he had her on the defensive.

"Is it? I'm pretty good at reading people, especially when they seem to have a one-track mind."

She shot him a dismissive look. "You don't know anything about my mind. Just because you're a writer doesn't give you the right to psychoanalyze me."

Stuart's head snapped back as though he had been hit in the face. "You have a good point there. Maybe I'm misjudging you. Just seems like I keep getting the brush-off when I'm trying to be friendly."

"Well, maybe you should stop trying so hard," she tossed back at him. "I'm sure there are other women in town you can strike up a conversation with. But right now I happen to be busy doing my job. If that somehow offends you, I can't do anything about it."

"No, I suppose you can't," Stuart said, deciding to cut this short before saying something he couldn't take back. "I'll let you get back to it and try not to bother you anymore."

He waited for a second or two, as if to see if she would try to get the last word. But there was no come-back. Apparently she was satisfied that she could declare victory over him.

Stuart knew this was a losing battle. And since he didn't like to lose, he saw no reason to torture either of them further. He turned and headed for the door.

Madison watched as he was leaving. She had a mind to call him back, air out some of their differences, but thought better. What was there to say, really? He seemed like a nice guy and was certainly very good-looking. But that didn't mean they had to be friends.

Especially since it wasn't what she wanted. Not when his presence made her feel unexpectedly giddy and nervous. She was still trying to put past regrets behind her.

She sipped more coffee and turned back to the book. Suddenly it became more laborious to read than ever.

She wondered how much Stuart Kendall had to do with that.

That night, after tucking the girls into bed, Stuart stretched out on the living room sectional and video-chatted with Holly on his iPad.

"Hey, sis."

She flashed him a big smile on a beautiful face that reminded him of their mother's. "Back at you, big brother. Or maybe I should say lean and mean brother of mine."

He chuckled. "Whatever works. How's the wedding planning going?"

"Great, although it's much more work than I thought it would be. How are the girls?"

"Growing up way too fast," he said honestly. "I know they're only seven, nearly eight, but next thing you know, they'll be eighteen. I don't even want to think about them dating and all that."

Holly laughed. "It's an inevitable part of life. You'll get used to it when the time comes."

"Yeah, we'll see about that." Stuart paused thoughtfully. "So what's the deal with your old friend, Madison?" He already had a pretty good idea, but he still wanted to try to gain a little added insight from Holly.

"Why, did she say something?" Holly's black eyes grew wide.

"Actually, it's just the opposite. She hasn't said enough," he complained. "I've tried to be there if she needed someone to help her get acclimated to Portland, since she was once your friend and all. But she clearly isn't interested in being friendly with me."

"Sorry to hear that," Holly said. "But it's understandable. She's probably feeling a little weird right now, knowing that her ex-fiancé is my current fiancé and that we're about to walk down the aisle. You're my brother, and she probably sees that as an extension of me."

"But I thought you said things were cool between the two of you when she left Houston?" Stuart asked.

"They were—are.... But that doesn't mean there aren't still hurt feelings. She probably needs a period of adjustment to fully accept the reality that Anderson and I are together."

"So during this adjustment, am I supposed to just avoid her? Or risk being shot down every time I attempt to engage her in some conversation?"

"Don't avoid her," Holly stressed. "Madison is really a nice person to get to know, just as you are. Give her some time to come around. My sense is that she could use a friend like you there, and she'll come to realize that, if she hasn't already."

"I doubt that she has yet," Stuart said with a little chuckle. "But I'll take your advice."

"That's what little sisters are for," she told him. "You two will be best buds, and maybe even more, before you know it."

"Let's just stick to best buds right now, if it ever happens. I'm not looking for romance. Been there, done that and you see where it's gotten me."

"It's gotten you two beautiful, precious little angels who I'm sure you wouldn't trade for the world," Holly said.

"Very true," he conceded. He couldn't imagine his life without Carrie and Dottie.

"So let's not allow Fawn to spoil that any or keep you from finding someone right to share your life with."

"I'll keep that in mind," he said. That didn't mean he was anywhere close to being ready to throw himself back into the dating game. And certainly not with Madison, who obviously had her own demons she was busy wrestling. Stuart eyed his sister. "At least you've found someone to love you. I'll settle for that for the time being."

"You can be so sweet at times," Holly said, blushing.

"Just at times?" he teased her.

"How about the majority of the time?"

"I'll go with that and not press my luck."

She laughed. "Good answer."

Stuart laughed, too, feeling better about things now.

Chapter 3

It was the night of Valentine's Day, and Madison was visiting her next-door neighbor Jacinta Poole. She and Jacinta had become good friends in recent weeks and Madison welcomed having a female friendship in Portland.

Jacinta was a year older and divorced. She was a professor of liberal arts at Portland State University and a longtime resident of Portland. Jacinta handed Madison a goblet of wine and the two sat at the table in the breakfast nook.

"Thanks for inviting me over," Madison said as she reached for the glass.

"I figured you could use some company," Jacinta said, brushing her Senegalese twists to one side of her head. "This is the day your ex is marrying your friend, right?"

"Yep, as far as I know." Madison gave her a thoughtful look. She had poured out her heart to Jacinta last month, expressing both sorrow and relief that her life was headed in a different direction. Now that her ex, Anderson, had made it official with Holly, it truly was time to put this behind her once and for all. After all, why should the two of them be happy and not her? She deserved to find a man who could truly appreciate her.

Jacinta seemed to read her mind. "Don't let it weigh you down, girl. If he chose to marry someone else, that's on him, not you."

"You're right," Madison agreed. "Guess it really hit home now that there's no turning back." Not that she had seriously considered going back to him since the moment things soured between them. She had too much self-respect to want to be with someone who couldn't and wouldn't commit to her.

"Honestly, I wish I'd known before I walked down the aisle that my ex would turn out to be a jerk," Jacinta said with a laugh. "Believe me, I would've run in the other direction as fast as I could."

Madison couldn't help but laugh. "Guess it really is better to avert disaster before it happens."

"That's what I'm talking about," Jacinta said. "This is a day for you to celebrate that you avoided what could have been the biggest mistake of your life."

"You're so right."

They clinked glasses to toast the moment.

"You're in the right city to find a real man," Jacinta said. "Portland is swarming with eligible bachelors."

"Oh, really?" In fact, Madison recalled reading something once about Portland being ranked as the first or second city in the country with the most single men. She couldn't help but think of Stuart as one of those eligible men. Or was he spoken for? Holly had suggested months ago that he was still dealing with his ex-wife who left him. Was that still the case?

"Some of them just happen to teach at PSU," Jacinta told her. "I'd be happy to introduce you around."

"Though the idea is tempting," Madison said, "right now, I think I'd rather let him come to me than go after him."

"Okay, I can respect that," Jacinta said. "Especially since I'm kind of in the same boat."

Madison chuckled. "Didn't I see you come home the other night with a good-looking guy?"

"Yes, I'm seeing someone," Jacinta admitted, "but it's pretty casual and I think we both know it's going nowhere in the long run. And, really, that's just fine right now, since I'm way too busy to become too emotionally invested in a man."

Madison wondered what her excuse was. She'd love to become emotionally involved with a man, but only if he would truly appreciate her, unlike Anderson. She just wasn't sure such a man existed. At least not in her universe.

She would simply have to bide her time and not put

herself out there only to get nothing but heartbreak in return.

"Let me refill your wine," Jacinta said, "and we can watch a DVD."

Madison smiled. "Sounds like a plan." It certainly beat sitting alone at home, with only a stack of books to review as her constant companion. She hoped that maybe by next Valentine's Day she would have someone in her life to share the joys of romance.

Stuart watched gleefully as the girls played with Grace in the park. She had a way with them, and he had no doubt that someday Grace would be a fine mother to her own children. He only wished Dottie and Carrie had a real mother around who they could count on to be there day in and day out. In spite of them being well-adjusted and seemingly content with their real mother long out of the picture, he still felt that maternal affection was something all children needed. But he was doing his best to try to be everything they needed with some help from Grace.

They were two weeks removed from a trip to Houston where they had attended Holly's wedding. Carrie and Dottie had served as flower girls and Holly was every bit the blushing bride. Anderson seemed to love her dearly and had been fully accepted into the family.

Stuart thought about his father and was glad that they'd had some time to visit while they were in Houston for the wedding. They had never been as close as he would have liked, as both were bullheaded at times and not always on the same page. But things had been improving lately between them. Both had lost someone dear to them, albeit in totally different circumstances, giving them common ground.

The fact that his father adored Dottie and Carrie went a long way in Stuart's book, as they needed their grandfather as much as he needed them.

Stuart wondered how long it would be before Holly gave his girls a cousin or two. He had no doubt that Holly wanted a family, and Anderson seemed of the same mind.

It made Stuart consider the possibility of one day giving Carrie and Dottie siblings. He was sure they would love that. So would he. Of course, he would first need a woman in his life who felt the same way. Neither seemed on the horizon at the moment. But he had decided to try to keep his mind open, even though Fawn had done her best to turn him off women forever.

Stuart snapped out of his reverie when Dottie tugged on his hand. "Come play with us, Daddy," she pleaded.

He smiled. "Are you sure I wouldn't be in the way?"

"I'm sure." She giggled. "Plus Grace said she has to leave soon to study."

"Well, in that case, I'll be happy to fill in for her," he said enthusiastically. He allowed her to take him by the hand and lead him over to where Carrie and Grace were.

On Monday morning in the first week of March, Madison was at her desk working on a review when Giselle knocked on the open door and entered.

"I see you're busy as usual," she said.

Madison didn't deny it. Her work was the perfect way to keep her mind occupied. "I like to make my deadlines."

"And you always do." Giselle sat down in a chair beside the desk. "I loved the review you wrote on Linda Bloom's latest romance."

"She's a great writer," Madison said.

"I agree," Giselle said. "And it doesn't hurt that she includes plenty of passion in her novels for folks who aren't getting enough in their real lives."

Madison batted her lashes. "Excuse me?"

"Sorry if I offended you," Giselle said sincerely. "That wasn't my intention. But it's obvious that you and I are very much alike—burying ourselves in work and fitness while not having much of a love life, if any. If I'm way off base—"

"You're not," Madison admitted. "My social life is pretty much nonexistent these days—by choice."

"I'm sure there's a story there," Giselle said hopefully.

Madison sighed, not wanting to go there. "Yeah, isn't there always?" She paused before saying, "I love my job, and if it can sometimes act as a substitute for real-life romance, then so be it."

"My sentiments exactly," Giselle said, smiling. "Actually, I've got a new assignment for you."

"Oh…" Madison wondered if Giselle would take advantage of her being a workaholic. Should she be flattered or insulted?

"Yes, I'd like you to interview Stuart Kendall for our May issue."

"Me?" Madison hadn't meant for it to sound like a question. Or like this was new territory for her, which it wasn't. She had done her fair share of interviews with authors in Houston.

"Yes, you," Giselle said. "You said you know him, right?"

"I know his sister, but him, not so well," Madison said.

"Well, here's your chance to get to know him better," Giselle told her wryly. "His book, *An Act of Murder,* will be released in May in paperback. It'll be a great feature on a local bestselling author and single dad."

Madison did not disagree that it would be a good article for the magazine. She just wasn't sure she was the best person to do it. Especially since things between her and Stuart hadn't exactly been cordial, which was totally her fault. It might make him less likely to want her to interview him.

"I'd love to do it," she offered halfheartedly, "but I'm really swamped with books to review and a story I'm working on for my column…"

"So I'll reassign some of your reviews," Giselle said. "And you can shorten your column if you need to. I just think that you're the perfect person to interview Stuart and maybe get inside his head to see how on earth he manages to balance a successful career with a home life of raising two little girls. I think our readers would eat up this piece."

Madison had a feeling this wasn't something she could turn down, even if she still had reservations about approaching Stuart after giving him the brush-off. But, after all, she really was sincere about wanting to put the past to rest. So forcing herself to socialize with Holly's brother without getting bent out of shape was a good place to put that to the test. The fact that it was in a professional capacity meant there would be no added pressure on either of them to make it personal.

"I'll be happy to interview Stuart Kendall," she told her boss. "Assuming he's willing. I know some authors prefer to let their words speak for them."

"From what I've heard and seen for myself, Stuart's not likely to pass on the interview. Especially since you're someone he knows, even if not too well," Giselle said confidently.

Madison made herself smile, while the thought of getting together with him made her heart race for some reason. "I'll try."

Giselle smiled back and got to her feet. "Great. I'll set it up."

"Actually, I'd like to set it up myself," Madison said, not wanting Stuart to somehow feel that he'd been blind-sided into doing an interview with her. "We both ride our bikes in the same area. I'm sure I'll run into him, and I can approach the subject then."

"That's fine," Giselle agreed. "Keep me posted."

She left and Madison thought about seeing Stuart again and how both of them might react to it. *I have to remain coolheaded and let him see more of the real me,* she thought, while hoping that she hadn't already blown the opportunity.

Chapter 4

On Wednesday, after taking the girls to school, Stuart drove home in his gray Mercedes. He put the dishes in the dishwasher and did a little writing before getting on his bicycle for a few miles of riding. It was the perfect escape from the hard work that had made him a bestseller.

It was a far cry from the early days when writing was strictly a part-time endeavor, and he had to make a living doing the best he could with various jobs. But things began to go his way following his first bestseller a few years ago. After that, he never looked back as far as money was concerned. He'd made wise investment choices and set up trust funds for both girls so they would never have to do without.

The one thing he knew money could not buy them

was the love of a mother. Stuart wished he had never gotten mixed up with Fawn, save for the two girls they'd brought into this world.

He rode his bike up the hill easily and was on his way down the other side, staying in the bicycle lane, when he spotted another cyclist ahead of him. It didn't take much for Stuart to recognize the rider as Madison Wagner. She was moving at a leisurely pace, seemingly enjoying the feel of the wind in her face and the beauty of her surroundings.

As though she had eyes in the back of her head, Madison turned once to look his way and slowed down at the bottom of the hill, as if to wait for him.

Maybe she thinks I'm someone else, he thought. *Hate to disappoint her and possibly ruin her day when she realizes she's going to cross paths with a Kendall.*

Given that their previous encounters had been less than ideal, Stuart almost considered turning around and going back up the hill to avoid another letdown. But that would be taking the easy way out. He was up for a challenge.

He cruised down the rest of the way before putting on the brakes, stopping just short of her. "Hey," he said casually.

"Hey." Madison gave him an uneasy smile. "Thought that might be you."

"And yet you still waited?" Stuart said, chuckling. "Sorry, couldn't resist."

"It's cool," she told him, realizing she hadn't made

it easy for him up to this point. "Look, we may have gotten off to the wrong start."

"You think?" he asked, raising a brow.

"I was just going through some things and you got caught up in it," Madison tried to explain.

"I understand," Stuart said, thinking back to Holly's wedding. "In any event, I am glad to see that we can at least carry on a conversation."

"So am I." She paused while eyeing the handsome man who was checking her out, too.

"Do you want to ride together for a bit?" he asked.

"Sure," she told him, welcoming the brief respite.

Stuart followed behind her, enjoying the view of her nice backside as she rode. "So what have you been up to lately?" Seemed like an easy enough way to get to know her, if she was open to it.

"Mostly work," Madison said. "How about you?"

"Same thing—along with trying to keep up with my girls."

"They're seven, right?" She seemed to recall Holly telling her that.

"They act more like seventeen sometimes," he said, chuckling. "They will be eight in June."

"That's nice."

Stuart could tell that she meant it; though he got the feeling she didn't have any kids. "I've been checking out your column and reviews when I've gotten the chance."

"Oh, really?" She looked at him, as they were now riding parallel in an area designated solely for bikes.

"Yeah," he admitted. "Apart from being a writer,

I'm an avid reader whenever time permits, which isn't often enough. You have some thoughtful reviews and interesting observations in your column."

"Thank you." Madison found herself blushing. Most writers she knew were too full of themselves to be bothered with reading anything but their own work. "I try to keep my reviews real and the column energetic so it doesn't put people to sleep."

"I think you've succeeded." Stuart grinned at her, wishing they had been able to compare notes sooner, but glad to see they were doing so now.

"I try my best." She held back and let him take the lead as they reentered the narrower bicycle path. This was the perfect segue to ask him what she wanted to. "I'd like to interview you...."

He glanced over his shoulder. "For the magazine?"

"Yes, a feature story in which you can tell readers about your writing, home life, kids," Madison said. "I'm sure it would be a hit for your fans and help new potential fans get to know you."

Stuart could not deny that she had a point. It hadn't been that long ago when no one was very much interested in his story. Least of all one of the hottest magazines in town. But that was then and this was now.

He did wonder about the timing, though. Had this just come up? Or had she been friendly all of a sudden as a way to butter him up for a damned interview?

Not that it mattered in the scheme of things. The reality was he saw this opportunity as a perfect icebreaker.

And it would allow him to dig a bit into her life as well, beyond what he already knew, which wasn't much.

"I'll be happy to give you an interview," Stuart told her with a smile.

"Wonderful." Madison breathed a sigh of relief. "How about tomorrow at lunchtime?"

He waited a beat as if to consider his busy schedule. Since the girls would be at school and his writing time was quite flexible, there was no problem meeting then, but he didn't want to seem overeager.

"Lunchtime sounds good," he said.

"Are you familiar with the Beef Barn on Fifth Avenue?" she asked.

"Yes, I've been there a couple of times."

"Great. I'll meet you there at one."

"It's a date," Stuart said.

After leaving Stuart, Madison rode home feeling as though she had pulled off a coup. He'd had every right to turn down the interview request, but he'd been surprisingly gracious. Perhaps he hadn't given her earlier brush-off much thought after it had happened. She was grateful for that.

She phoned Giselle with the news. "We're meeting tomorrow."

"That was quick," Giselle said.

"No time like the present," Madison said lightly as she sat on a porch step.

"I couldn't agree more. I'm sure it will be a nice piece on one of Portland's most eligible bestselling authors."

"Thanks for the vote of confidence," Madison said.

"My pleasure," Giselle told her. "That's what I'm here for."

Madison would remember that. But even without such encouragement from her boss, she felt she was more than up to the task of peering into Stuart's life and his success as an author. As for the eligible part, she supposed she could broach that, too, if only to see how he dealt with that as a single dad.

The next morning, Madison picked out a nice navy dress for the interview. After debating whether or not to put up her hair, she opted to leave it down. It seemed to suit her best. Last night she had done a little research on Stuart over the internet to help prepare for the interview. His wife had left him four years ago so he had to raise their children alone. And, apparently, he had done just that, with no indication that he had been involved with anyone else.

On the professional front, he had gone from midlist to bestseller status less than a decade ago. Now he seemed to have the Midas touch as a mystery novelist, two of which had been adapted to the screen.

Definitely gives me something to work with, Madison thought, while driving to the restaurant. *Now it's up to me to see what else I can draw out that readers will find interesting.*

Carrying her tablet, she walked into the restaurant at five minutes to one and immediately spotted Stuart in the waiting area.

He saw her, too, and walked up to her. "Hey."

"Hi," she said, trying hard not to stare too much, but finding it hard to resist. He stood there in a nice button-down shirt and tailored pants that looked good on him. She detected pleasant-smelling cologne, as well. "Hope you weren't waiting too long."

"Not at all," Stuart assured her, giving her the once-over. She looked great in her body-contouring dress. He proffered his arm when the hostess appeared. "Shall we?"

Madison followed Stuart to a table near the window with a view of the river.

"Would either of you like anything to drink?" the hostess asked.

"Red wine for me," Madison answered.

"I'll have the same," Stuart said.

They were handed menus and left to themselves.

After taking a glance at the offerings, Stuart turned his attention back to Madison. "So how do we do this? Multitask? Or get the bulk of the interview out of the way first and then eat?"

Madison smiled. "I think we can eat and talk, as I'm starved, if that's fine with you."

"More than fine," he assured her, looking again at the menu and back to Madison. "What do you recommend?" He was curious to see what her taste was in food.

"Hmm…" She looked over the choices, sensing she was being tested. "How about filet mignon, mashed sweet potatoes and mixed vegetables?"

Stuart grinned at her across the table. "Sounds good to me."

"Me, too," she said.

They ordered as the wine came.

Madison saw that as an excellent opportunity to get started and take mental notes in lieu of her iPad for the moment. "So what made you want to become a writer?" she asked.

Stuart had been asked this question often enough, and his response was usually pretty much the same. "I don't think there was ever a time when I wasn't a writer to one degree or another," he said over his wineglass. "I started writing stories as a boy and have never let up to this day."

Madison smiled. "Well, it looks like you found your calling early in life."

"I did. Of course, it took years to hone the craft and find the genre that worked best for me."

She sipped her wine. "That would be the mystery-thriller genre?"

"Yes," he said. "Before that I tried Western, science fiction and even mainstream before settling into thriller fiction."

"So what do you feel is the key thing that makes you such a great thriller writer?" Madison asked curiously.

"Good question," Stuart said, and thought about it. "I'd say the main thing has been reading lots of high-quality thriller fiction over the years to get a sense of what's being published successfully. This gave me a pretty good idea of what to do and what not to do in the genre."

"So you credit your contemporaries, at least in part, for your own success?"

"Yes, along with those who came before me," he pointed out. "Writers such as Dashiell Hammett, Robert Ludlum and Mickey Spillane, among others, influenced my own writing of crime fiction."

Madison took out her iPad and jotted this down. "You were inspired by some of the masters of mystery novels."

"Exactly."

"And now you've become a master in your own right."

Stuart laughed. "Well, I'm not sure about that. I think I'll probably always be a pupil of the genre. There's room to grow for every writer."

"And modest, too." She smiled.

"Just calling it like I see it," he insisted.

The food arrived and they both dug in.

"So what was it like to see two of your books go from print to the big screen?" Madison asked, taking a bite of mashed sweet potatoes. "I'm sure you must have been thrilled."

"To be honest with you," Stuart told her, "I didn't think either movie quite hit the mark of the books."

She arched a brow. "Really?"

He nodded. "When a 350-page book is turned into an hour-and-a-half movie, the integrity of the story is bound to suffer." He sliced through the tender filet mignon. "But I understand the nature of the business called Hollywood and, as such, am thankful that someone thought enough of my books to want to make them into movies. My sister certainly loved them."

Stuart remembered as soon as he mentioned Holly that it was a sore spot with Madison. "I didn't mean—" he started.

"It's all right," Madison broke in. "I'm glad Holly enjoyed the movies." The last thing she wanted at this point was for him to feel that the subject of his sister— or Anderson, for that matter—was totally off-limits. Especially when they were meeting in a professional capacity and it was she who had brought up the movies.

Stuart felt relieved that this hadn't put a damper on the interview. "My guess is that she would've loved the movies even if they were total crap, because they were based on my novels."

Madison chuckled. "You're probably right." She sliced into her steak thoughtfully. "How long does it take you to write a novel?"

"It depends on how much of a handle I have on the plot and what else is going on at the time," he explained. "But, in general, I'd say about four months."

"Wow. That's a pretty quick turnaround," Madison said. "No wonder you're so prolific."

He shrugged. "I guess it's easy when you don't have much of a social life outside of your kids."

"I'm sure they can be a handful at times, though adorable day in and day out."

"Couldn't have said it better myself," Stuart said,

dabbing a napkin at the corners of his mouth. "I can't imagine what I'd ever do without them."

Though Madison suspected this would be a difficult subject, she felt obligated to bring it up anyway. "I read about your ex-wife abandoning you and your daughters."

"It's true." He knew it had made the local news at the time because of his celebrity. It hadn't helped that his ex seemed perfectly willing to exploit the situation for financial gain and attention. "She met someone passing through and decided to run off with him and that was that."

"Ouch!"

"Yeah, I know." Stuart finished off his filet mignon, frowning. "Never saw it coming till it was too late to do a damned thing about it. But I did file for divorce as soon as possible."

"I can't say I blame you. For a woman to do such a thing—especially to her children—is unconscionable."

"You're right, it is," he said. "But we're managing to get by on our own. Her loss."

Madison was inclined to agree now that she'd had a chance to talk to him. Still she wondered if his girls were really doing that well without a mother in their lives. Or had he been able to make up for her absence through his own love and devotion?

"It's quite impressive that you've gone it alone these past years raising your daughters, yet you still managed to keep churning out bestsellers," she said. "How have you done it?"

"You do what you have to do," Stuart responded candidly. "As a father, I owe it to my daughters to let them know I will always be there for them no matter what. I also know that I have to keep up my career to provide for them and myself. It has been a juggling act at times, but I wouldn't have it any other way right now."

Madison took that to mean he wasn't interested in romance at this point in his life. Or was she simply implanting her own thoughts into his? "Maybe someday you'll find another woman who can give you that balance in life and who can be a mother figure your daughters look up to."

"That's certainly possible," he allowed. "I'm in no hurry, though. If it happens, it happens. If not, well, I won't have to worry about yet another disappointment."

"Good point," she had to agree. "Even if it's terrible to have to think in those terms."

"I wish it weren't the case," he said. More than she knew. But the baggage of betrayal and abandonment did that to you, no matter how much you tried to erase it from your mind totally. Stuart regarded Madison, remembering that she could relate in some ways. "Now that we've gone through my life and times, I'd like to know more about yours—"

Her eyes widened uncomfortably. "I'm not the one being interviewed."

"I'm not interviewing you," he stressed. "I just want to talk about what brought you to this point. Obviously, our lives have intersected in a way that was pretty much beyond either of our control. Seems like a good time to put it on the table."

As much as she wanted to disagree, Madison could not. He had opened up himself to her, over and beyond what was necessary for the interview. So why not return the favor?

"All right," she said, meeting his gaze. "I'm sure you know all the dirty details of my ex, Anderson, calling off our engagement, only to wind up marrying your sister."

"Actually, I don't know the dirty details of it," Stuart pointed out. "Just the basic facts. As I understand it, your relationship with Anderson ended well before Holly ever came into the picture."

"That's true," Madison confessed as she took a sip of wine. "I honestly never thought I'd ever see Anderson again until I found out he was dating Holly. Before that, I only had the memories of him backing out of an engagement so he could 'find himself.' And then, there he was...."

"It must have really thrown you for a loop."

"That's putting it mildly."

"And you came here because you couldn't deal with—"

"No," Madison cut him off. "I came here because I was offered a good job and a chance to start over. In my heart of hearts, I was over Anderson the moment he walked out on our future. While it may have taken a period of adjustment when he resurfaced, I am over it now. And I don't blame Holly for any of this."

"You sure about that?" The one thing he did not want was to see her and his sister at odds for the rest of their lives. It wouldn't be fair to either of them.

"I'm sure," she responded. "She was entitled to find love whenever it found her, which happened when Anderson came into her world. Yes, it did mean that our friendship suffered a bit, naturally, but I really want Holly to be happy and her marriage to work."

"Maybe you should tell her that sometime," Stuart said.

"I already have," Madison said. "But I'll do so again, so that we're clear on it."

He nodded, happy to hear her say that. Though he completely understood her position on this whole situation, Stuart also believed Holly missed the connection with her friend and would welcome the opportunity to jump-start things.

Beyond that, he was intrigued by the woman sitting before him now that he had begun to peel away the layers of defenses she had built around herself.

"So when will this feature appear in the magazine?" he asked, getting back to more comfortable territory.

"The May issue," Madison told him, "which actually comes out next month. I'll run it by you before turning in the final draft."

"Sounds good," he said. "I'll be sure to post info about it to my fans on Twitter and Facebook. They usually love these kinds of things."

"I think it's more like they love their writers and whatever comes with the territory."

Stuart laughed. "Yeah, that, too."

Madison chuckled.

She asked a few more pointed questions about his career, developing plot ideas and upcoming books before they ended the interview.

It surprised Madison that she had felt so comfortable talking to Stuart about herself. Was it his ability to draw that out of her? Or was it something else?

Chapter 5

That night, Madison worked on the feature over a glass of wine. She was happy to have gotten so much information from Stuart. Since he hadn't specifically told her that anything he'd said was off-limits, she assumed she was free to use everything they talked about to show how he'd shaped his career while doing a delicate balancing act as a single and doting father of two little girls.

It was definitely going to be an uplifting, cutting-edge piece. Giselle would hopefully approve and assign her more interviews with high-profile authors in the future.

I'm definitely up for the challenge, she thought.

But back to the interview. She planned to contact Stuart about a photograph to accompany the feature.

Since she believed he would most likely appear on the front cover, he would need to have their photographer take his picture.

Something told her this would be no problem. For one, he was drop-dead handsome. And for another, Stuart seemed cool and confident where it came to his looks and would likely want to do his part to enhance the interview.

The following day, Madison went with her friend Jacinta to the Rose City Spa for a full treatment of massage, facial, manicure and pedicure.

"I'm so glad you talked me into this," Madison told Jacinta. They were both in the middle of an organic facial—including cleansing, toning and exfoliation—with a facial massage and treatment mask.

"I knew you would love it," she responded. "I try to come here at least once a month to get myself back together."

"I can see why," Madison said. She closed her eyes and allowed the experience to soak in. It was her first time at a spa in Portland and definitely wouldn't be the last.

"Might as well be as beautiful as you can be, girl-friend," Jacinta said. "Who knows what hot guy might be waiting around the corner to sweep you off your feet? No harm in trying to look tantalizing."

Madison laughed. "I don't know about tantalizing a guy, but it sure makes me feel great."

"You haven't felt anything yet," she said. "Just wait

till we do the Swedish massage and body sculpting and skin tightening treatments!"

"I can hardly wait," Madison said truthfully.

"I'd still love to introduce you to one of my single colleagues at the university," Jacinta said. "I know that any of them would fall head over heels for you."

"Thanks, but I'd rather stay on my own for now." Madison wondered if she really believed her words. Hadn't she let go of the past? If so, maybe it was time to see who might be out there for her.

For whatever reason, Stuart Kendall came to mind. She didn't put much into the thought, knowing that they were just getting to know one another as friends. Looking beyond that was foolish, especially when Stuart seemed like he was perfectly content with writing and his girls. There didn't seem to be any room in his life these days for anyone else.

Stuart sat with the other parents in the auditorium as Carrie and Dottie took part in the school play. They had taken their roles seriously, practicing at home with Grace, who had shown great patience in supporting them.

But he knew that support wouldn't last forever. Sooner or later Grace would move on with her life and he would have to get a new nanny for the girls. Stuart dreaded the thought, as he didn't feel it was healthy for Dottie and Carrie to go through too many nannies. What they truly needed was a mother in their lives.

But not their real mother—he doubted they would

ever see her again. Rather, they needed a replacement mom who could give them everything their own mother never had. Was it wishful thinking on his part, or could it actually happen sooner than later?

Of course for it to be possible at all, he needed to find a special connection with a woman. Though it hadn't happened since Fawn left, Stuart was an eternal optimist. Why couldn't he still meet his great love who would respect his children and not be overwhelmed by his career?

Or am I just deluding myself? he wondered, as a slice of pessimism coursed through him.

When he suddenly thought about Madison Wagner, Stuart smiled. He wasn't sure if it was the thought of her beautiful face and hot figure. Or the fact that they had finally managed to break the ice and it now seemed like they might actually get along.

He wondered what Carrie and Dottie would think of her. Maybe one day he would find out. But only if there was a chance that they could start something that wouldn't be here one day and gone the next. He would not subject his girls to anything less than a potentially serious relationship with someone. As a father, he had to put their interests over anyone else's. Including his own.

Stuart heard clapping and realized that the play had just ended. He joined in on the clapping as the young actors held hands and bowed together to the applause. He took pictures with his cell phone of Dottie and Carrie with their colorful costumes and thousand-watt smiles, wanting the memories to last a lifetime.

* * *

That evening, Stuart met with his agent and friend, Lyle Creighton, at a lounge on Hawthorne Boulevard. The two had worked together since Stuart sold his first book after others had turned down the chance to represent him. Though he had since been pursued by agents with powerful agencies, Stuart chose to stand by the agent who had stood by him and helped him become a bestselling author.

He told Lyle about the interview he gave to *Rose Petals*.

"That's great," Lyle said. "After that superb review they did on your latest book, this fits right in for maximizing your exposure in the Portland area, and elsewhere."

"My thoughts exactly," Stuart said. It also appeared as though the interview had paid off with Madison, as Stuart had a feeling that they had taken a step forward in getting closer, whatever that meant.

"So how are those little girls of yours doing?" Lyle asked.

"They're doing well. Both had starring roles in the school play today."

Lyle chuckled. "Hey, maybe someday they can wind up with roles in one of the movies made from your books."

"You never know," Stuart said, though he wasn't overly enthusiastic about either of his girls going into show business.

* * *

A few days had passed since Madison had interviewed Stuart, yet it somehow seemed longer. She fine-tuned the article and was ready to send it to him for approval, having already gotten the thumbs-up from her boss. It was Madison's first cover piece since coming to work for the magazine, and she was excited about it. She hoped that the visibility would shine a light on not only Stuart, but herself, as well.

She dialed Stuart's cell phone number. It rang a few times before a girl picked up, catching Madison off guard.

"Hello," Madison said, unsure which twin it was. "May I speak to Stuart, please?"

"He's playing around with my sister," the girl said. "Just a minute."

Madison listened as she called out, "Daddy!"

In a moment, Stuart came on the phone. "Hello."

"Hi, it's Madison," she said, almost feeling like they were strangers.

"Hey there." Stuart's voice rose. "Nice to hear from you."

Was he merely being polite? Or did he really mean it?

"Hope I didn't catch you at a bad time," she said.

"You didn't," he replied. "I was just having some fun with the girls."

"I've wrapped up the piece on you and wanted you to take a look at it first to see if I missed anything or there's something you want removed," she told him.

"I'll be happy to look at," Stuart said in a friendly tone. "I'm sure, though, that you did a good job."

"That confident, are we?" Madison asked, half jokingly.

"Yeah. I've read your material. You're good."

"Thank you." She blushed, hoping he didn't change his opinion once he read the article. "Anyway, I'd like to email it to you."

"Good idea." He gave her his email address.

"Also, since this will be a cover story, we'd like to send over our photographer to take your picture," Madison told him. "I know you're a busy man, but it won't take long."

"No problem," he said. "Let's see…how does two o'clock tomorrow afternoon sound?"

"I'll check with him, but I'm sure he can accommodate the time that's best for you."

"Good," Stuart said.

Madison switched gears. "So that was your daughter who answered the phone…."

"Yes, Carrie."

"She has a cute voice."

"So does her sister, though I can't always tell the difference," Stuart said.

"Well let's hope you do before they turn eighteen," Madison teased.

He chuckled. "Yeah, I know. Hopefully that time won't get here too fast."

"Hopefully not. Anyway, I'll let you get back to them."

"Thanks for calling," Stuart said. "Speak to you soon."

After she disconnected, Madison found herself hoping that they really would speak again soon. Even so, she tempered her enthusiasm, realizing that both of them would need to open up more if they were to speak more often. Was he up to the task?

Was she?

The next day, Stuart took the girls to school. He gave them both a kiss on the cheek before sending them off to join their friends.

On the way home, he thought about Madison calling yesterday. It really was nice to hear her voice, which had a pleasant inflection to it. Maybe even sexy in a way.

He had read the piece on him and thought she had done a fabulous job. She had her own way with words, and she seemed to have covered the bases readers wanted to know about an author.

She made me look good, something all authors want, he thought.

Even Lyle thought the article was wonderful and hoped to use it in future negotiations.

Could be that Madison had become somewhat of a good luck charm to him.

At two o'clock, the photographer showed up at Stuart's house. "I'm John Gregg," he said. There was a camera bag strapped across his shoulder.

"Nice to meet you, John," Stuart said, looking up at

the twenty-something tall man with long hair. "Come on in."

"Thanks." They stepped into the foyer. "I have to say I'm a big fan of yours."

"Good to know," Stuart said politely.

"So where would you like to do this?"

"In my study." Stuart led the way.

"I should only need a few pictures and then I'll be out of your hair."

Stuart was counting on that, as he had to pick up the girls shortly and run some errands. He had dressed casually for the photographs, since that was how he would normally dress when writing.

The photo shoot was over in less than ten minutes.

"I'm sure Madison will let you know which photo the editor settles on for the cover," John said. "But I don't think you can go wrong with any of them."

Stuart smiled. "I'll wait to hear from Madison."

He saw the photographer out and then grabbed his keys and left, knowing that between the girls and errands, there was still plenty to do before the day was through. He wondered if any woman would be able to handle a busy single writer with two growing girls.

Or was that too much to ask?

Chapter 6

Stuart was in his study writing when the phone rang. He grabbed it off the desk and saw that it was his father.

"Hey, Dad."

"Hey yourself," Robert Kendall said. "I was just reading the article about you in the magazine you sent. Nice piece."

"Thanks." Stuart smiled. Compliments rarely came from his father, as that just didn't seem to be in his DNA. At least not where it concerned Stuart. He believed that, for whatever reason, Holly had always received more of their father's praise. Yet Stuart knew that deep down inside he had earned his old man's respect, whether he showed it or not. "Most of the credit goes to the interviewer," he told him.

"I doubt it," his father said. "She could only work with what she had. In this case, it was you."

"Good point." Stuart had clearly caught him in a generous mood and wouldn't complain one bit. "It seemed like a great opportunity for some added exposure."

"I agree. One can never have enough of that, especially in your business where there aren't enough truly great writers."

Where is this coming from? Stuart asked himself. Great writer? He had expected a cursory commendation, but not this. He wondered if Holly had talked to their father, which would explain his behavior given the soft spot he had for her. Stuart had sent her a copy of the magazine as well and, as expected, she had loved it.

"I appreciate the compliment," he told his father. "I've certainly paid my dues and I'm happy to be where I am today."

"As you should be," Robert said. "Same is true for your sister."

"I'm proud of her, too."

"You know, she's one up on you," Robert told him.

Stuart frowned. "What do you mean?"

"She finally found herself a man and is settling down," his father said. "And you, well…it's high time you got back with the program and found someone who can make you happy."

"I am happy," Stuart said uncomfortably. "I have the girls and my writing—"

"Right, but no one to cuddle up to at night. You deserve to be with a woman who won't stab you in the back. Don't be afraid to hop back in the saddle, son."

"I'm not afraid," Stuart said, trying to convince himself more than anything. "Yes, Fawn definitely left a sour taste in my mouth for relationships. But I'm still willing to put myself out there when the time is right."

"The time is right now," Robert told him bluntly. "Your girls need a mother figure in their lives so they don't think all women are like Fawn."

"I doubt they think that." He knew they had taken a liking to Grace and didn't feel she was anything like their mother. But they also thought of her more as a friend than a substitute mother.

"My point is that before you know it they'll be out the door and you'll be old like me, wondering where the years have gone," Robert said. "Find someone to love and, more importantly, to love you and the girls with all her heart, and it will make you complete."

"Like it did for Holly?" Stuart asked.

"Something like that," Robert responded. "I've never seen her so happy and I want to say the same thing about you."

"Got it," Stuart said and sucked in a breath. Even if he didn't necessarily like being pressured, he understood that his father meant well. "I'll see what I can do about that."

"Okay. And if you ever need to have some time away from the kids, send them down here to stay with their granddaddy."

"I'll keep that in mind," Stuart said, remembering

how much they had enjoyed visiting their grandfather and Holly in February. But he would never send them away to get rid of them while he focused on his romantic life. On the contrary, should he start dating anyone seriously, he would want her to be a big part of his girls' lives. They were a package deal.

The very notion made him think of Madison, even though they were just becoming friends. They had only gotten together once and that was for the interview. For all he knew, she didn't even like children. But she had mentioned that Carrie had a cute voice. Was that a good sign that she was amenable to being with someone with two irresistible daughters?

Madison dusted furniture while half watching the television. She was thinking about her big move to Portland and how things seemed to be falling into place now. The job was going well. She'd made a few friends and had even begun to venture out and discover some interesting things about the city and its surroundings. She loved that there were competing rivers and the majestic Cascade Mountains, with the Pacific Ocean and the beach less than a two-hour drive away. It seemed as if there were almost too many things to do. If only she had the time to do them all.

Or had someone special to do them with.

Someone like Stuart might be nice, she thought. He had offered to partner with her for bicycling. Maybe she would take him up on it if he was serious.

He could even bring along his girls on their bikes, if

he wanted to. So what if people mistakenly thought they were a happy family? She certainly didn't want to give a false impression, but she couldn't be blamed if his ex-wife had chosen to look elsewhere for companionship.

The chime of her cell phone snapped Madison out of her daydreaming. The caller ID showed it was Stuart.

She smiled at the thought of hearing his voice. He was probably calling to talk about the magazine, which officially came out this week, though he had received contributor copies last week.

"Hello there," she said softly.

"Hi," he said. "Are you busy?"

"Nothing I can't finish later."

"I wanted to thank you for the interview. Everyone who's read it, including my father, seemed to think you did a hell of a job making me look good."

She chuckled. "Uh, I think you did that all by yourself."

"I doubt it," Stuart said. "You have a way of making people feel comfortable opening up."

"I could say the same thing about you," she surprised herself by admitting.

"I'll take that as a compliment."

"You should."

"All right, I will." He gave a little laugh. "I was thinking, now that the issue is out successfully, we should celebrate."

"Oh?" Madison switched the phone to her other ear. "What did you have in mind?"

"Do you like jazz?"

"I love jazz," she told him. She had a huge list of songs by the jazz greats on her iPad and computer.

"Great! I have a buddy, Chad, who is a jazz musician. He plays at the Rooster Club down on Broadway," Stuart said. "I think we should check it out."

Was this a date? she wondered. Or was it a get-together between business associates? Either way, she was up for it.

"Yes, let's do it."

"May I pick you up at six?" he asked.

"Six is fine." She gave him her address and they talked a little more before she cut it short. Though she enjoyed talking to him, Madison needed some time to shower and get ready for their outing. It would be her first time going to a jazz club since she'd moved to Portland and she honestly couldn't think of anyone she would rather go with.

Stuart made arrangements for Grace to stay with the girls till he got back. He was excited about this opportunity to take Madison to hear Chad do his thing. Moreover, it gave them another chance to spend some time together and get to know one another.

He parked in front of the town house, went up to the entrance and rang the bell. After a moment or two, the door opened and Madison was standing there.

"Hello," she said with an effervescent smile.

"Hey." Stuart took a good look at her and his jaw practically dropped. She wore a one-shoulder draped fuchsia dress that accentuated her amazing figure, along with matching stylish platform pumps. Her long hair rested on one side of her beautiful face. Whatever perfume she was wearing, it worked its magic on him. "You look incredible," he told her.

"Thanks," Madison said. She was equally taken with Stuart, who looked sexy in a navy blue suit and black shoes. She loved the woodsy scent of his cologne, as well. "I could say the same thing about you."

He blushed. He usually took comments about his good looks in stride. But it actually meant something coming from her. "Are you ready?"

"Yes, all set." She was eager to spend some time with him, without work matters getting in the way.

Stuart grinned. "Then let's go enjoy some music."

He opened the passenger door of his Mercedes and she got in.

"Nice ride," she couldn't help but say.

"Gets me where I want to go," Stuart said simply.

"So does your bike," Madison pointed out. "But it's not quite as luxurious."

He chuckled. "True, but it sure can get you through tight spaces when there's a traffic jam."

She laughed. "Yes, I've noticed that too since being here."

"If you stay long enough, you'll see a lot more of what makes Portland such a special place to live."

"Really?" Madison faced his profile. She couldn't help but wonder if that included seeing more of him. And maybe even his little girls.

"Yes," Stuart said.

"Such as?"

"Better to keep you in suspense so you can enjoy it as time progresses," he told her deftly.

She frowned playfully. "Not fair."

He laughed. "Okay, I'll play fair. There's the Rose Festival, the Lan Su Chinese Garden, the Oregon Museum of Science and Industry, the art museum, the jazz festival, the Bridgetown Comedy Festival, the farmer's markets, the Cinco de Mayo Fiesta. I could go on and on…."

Madison chuckled. "Guess there is a lot to see and do."

"You bet," Stuart said, gazing at her. "I assume you plan to stick around for a while?"

"Of course," she responded without hesitation. "I love it here and have no desire to go anywhere else."

He smiled, comforted at the thought. "Good to know."

"So does this mean you'll be showing me some of these places and events?" Madison asked.

"I'd be happy to," he promised.

Madison took that as a good sign that tonight could be the start of something exciting.

Stuart followed Madison into the Rooster Club, where he had reserved a front-table seat. He pulled out her chair for her.

"Thank you," she told him. She had to get used to a man being a gentleman.

Stuart sat down. "What would you like to drink?"

"I'll have chardonnay," Madison responded, not bothering to look at the menu.

"So be it." He ordered two glasses of chardonnay and then saw Chad coming their way.

"I see you made it," Chad said.

"It was a good time to catch your act again," Stuart said.

"And you brought along a friend."

"Madison, this is Chad Schmidt," Stuart said. "Chad, Madison Wagner."

"Hi," she said.

"Nice to meet you," Chad said, shaking her hand. "Glad you were able to talk this dude into coming to hear my music."

She smiled. "I think it was more the other way around."

"Well, you two enjoy the show," Chad said. "I'll try not to miss any notes."

"You do that," Stuart kidded.

Soon the lights lowered and Chad, accompanied by a saxophonist and guitarist, began belting out some of the jazz classics.

"He's great, isn't he?" Stuart whispered to Madison.

"Yes, he's fantastic," she said. She was sure her sister would love this and made a mental note to take her there when Bianca came to visit. "How long have you two known each other?"

"A few years." He didn't want to explain just yet how he had met Chad during the darkest time in his life.

"Has he had any of his music recorded?" Madison asked.

"As a matter of fact he has," Stuart said. "He's working on getting an album out by the end of the year."

"That's fantastic," Madison said. "I'll have to download it onto my iPod when it's available."

"He'll like that," Stuart said. He liked it, too. It spoke well of her character that she was willing to support a friend of his.

They both looked toward the stage as Chad introduced his next song, before saying, "We have a dance floor and I don't see anyone using it. Maybe now is the time to bring that lady on your arm up here and do some nice slow-dancing to this song that's perfect for lovers—or friends with benefits…."

That last comment drew a laugh from the audience, including Madison and Stuart.

"So what do you say?" Stuart asked her. "We may not be lovers or friends with benefits, but I'd still love to have this dance with you."

Madison felt a rush of warmth envelope her at the thought of their bodies pressing close on the dance floor.

She smiled. "Let's go for it, if you think you've got it in you."

He chuckled. "Oh, I think I can hold my own."

Standing, Stuart took Madison's hand and joined a few other couples on the dance floor. While Chad began singing "Wave," Madison moved easily into Stuart's arms, which he wrapped around her, bringing them closer together. It was a surprisingly nice fit.

She put her arms on Stuart's shoulders as they moved around slowly to the romantic tune.

Does this feel as right to him as it does to me? Madison wondered. Or was the closeness she felt more a reflection of the wine and atmosphere?

"This was a good idea," Stuart whispered in her ear, having taken one of her hands as they moved.

Madison looked up at his face. "The jazz club or the dance?"

"Both. I'm definitely enjoying the evening on all fronts."

"Me, too." She wondered if he'd ever come here with his ex-wife. Or perhaps another woman.

Madison checked such thoughts, realizing none of that mattered. It wasn't as though they were dating or as if neither of them had a past.

Chad and the band finished the tune, and Madison hated that being in Stuart's capable arms had come to an end.

They sat down and had another drink while listening to more jazz songs.

"So what other writers have you interviewed since you've been in town?" Stuart asked during a break.

"Actually, you're my first one," Madison told him.

He grinned. "I'm honored."

"So am I. You were a great interview. In Houston, most times I had to practically shake the person to get something out of them. But you fed off everything I asked, and then some."

"That's because you asked all the right questions and were able to fill in the blanks on your own."

She smiled. "Guess we both made it work."

"I think that's a fair statement." He smiled at her.

"We'll have to do it again sometime," she threw out, hoping she wasn't being too forward.

"Anytime," he said. "I have a new novel coming out this fall, so that might be a good time to talk about it and whatever else I've got in the works."

"I'll plan on it then." Madison was certain that Giselle would be in favor of doing another interview with Stuart, especially given his popularity.

He smiled at her again, thinking it was becoming easier with every moment they spent together.

The band came back on stage and played one more set of classic jazz and a couple contemporary numbers.

Afterward, Stuart drove Madison home. He walked her to the door, wishing the night had not come to an end so soon.

"Hope you enjoyed the evening," he told her.

"I did," she said. She wondered if she should invite him in for a nightcap. But she thought better of it, figuring he needed to get home to his daughters.

"Well, thanks again for the interview and the company tonight," he said.

"It was my pleasure on both counts." Madison smiled brightly so he would know that she meant every word.

Stuart peered into her eyes for a long moment. "See you later," he finally said.

"Bye."

Madison went inside. *I actually thought he might kiss me,* she thought. Was that just wishful thinking, or was there actually a connection between them?

Madison had just kicked off her shoes when the doorbell rang. She thought it might be Stuart, and her heart skipped a beat.

Instead, it was Jacinta. "Hey, girl."

Madison hid her disappointment. "Hi."

"I couldn't help but notice that hunk of a man who just dropped you off."

He's hard not to notice, Madison thought.

"So...who is he?" Jacinta prodded.

"His name is Stuart. I did an interview on him for the magazine."

Jacinta put a hand to her mouth. "Oh, yeah. I read it. Stuart Kendall, the mystery writer. I'm surprised I didn't recognize him. He's one of my favorite authors. Are you two dating?"

"Not exactly," she said. "He invited me to see his friend play at the Rooster Club."

"Sounds pretty chummy to me."

"We're friends," Madison said, trying not to make anything more out of it. She knew Jacinta had a tendency to quickly draw the wrong conclusions.

"Well, maybe you can get your *friend* to autograph his latest book for me," Jacinta said.

"I can try."

"Cool." She scooted inside past Madison. "But first things first. I want to know the real story with what's going on between you and Mr. Bestselling Author...."

Madison chuckled. "You have a devious mind, girl."

"No, it's just curiosity from an admittedly nosey neighbor."

Madison did not really want to talk about it, but figured Jacinta would not go away till she did.

"I used to hang out with Stuart's sister in Houston," she said.

Jacinta cocked a brow. "Is that so?"

"Yes. So when I moved here, it was only natural that we would connect." She saw no reason to talk about the fact that it had gotten off to a rocky start.

"You're just full of surprises," Jacinta said. "And I thought you weren't in the market for a man."

Madison batted her eyes. "Who says I am?"

"The body language I picked up between you and Stuart made it clear."

Madison laughed. "I think you only saw what you wanted to see."

"Uh-uh," Jacinta said, snickering. "My eyesight is fine, thank you."

"Really, Stuart and I are just friends at this point."

"Aah, so you *are* interested in the man," Jacinta said.

"I didn't say that," Madison replied. She was clearly failing at trying to hide her emotions.

"You didn't have to. The man is hot, you're hot. Why not go for it and see where it leads?"

"Maybe so, maybe no. But right now, I'm going to bed. Alone."

Jacinta grinned. "I get the message. I'll see you

later." When she got to the door, she turned around and said, "Sweet dreams...."

"You, too," Madison said. She wondered if Stuart might be the one to make her dreams sweet.

Chapter 7

Stuart was in the park with Dottie, Carrie and Grace, riding their bikes. It was a warm day in the middle of April, perfect for riding. He trailed behind the three, keeping watch over them while everyone got their workout for the day.

He thought about how he had gone last week to the Rooster Club with Madison, then been ribbed about it the next day by Chad, who seemed to think they made the perfect couple. Stuart couldn't disagree with him, except for one little problem: they weren't seeing each other. In fact, they hadn't seen one another since that night and had only spoken once, briefly, when Madison phoned to say that sales of the magazine issue with him on the cover were going through the roof. He couldn't have been more pleased.

As for dating, the idea of a possible relationship with Madison certainly appealed to Stuart. They seemed to have chemistry, were both single and, as far as he knew, she was available. The main problem from his end was finding time, since so much of it seemed to be tied up in his kids and writing.

And what about Madison? he thought. Was she sufficiently over Anderson Gunn and willing to take a chance on another man?

If so, could I be the man to make her forget about him? Stuart wondered.

"Daddy, I'm tired," Dottie complained, bringing him back to reality.

"That means you're working those little muscles," he said lightly. "How about you, Carrie?"

"I'm fine," she said.

"So am I," Grace added. "I just wish I had the time to ride more often, especially with you guys."

"Can't we stop now?" Dottie said.

"All right, let's take a break before heading home. Then I'll let you girls decide where to go for lunch."

That perked them both up and he smiled, though he wasn't sure it was such a good idea to give them too much leeway or they'd end up eating nothing but junk food. It was times like these when he wished there was a woman in their lives who could cook and share the responsibility of tending to the girls' needs. Not to mention his needs as a man. He had loads of passion to give to the right woman.

It would happen when it did. In the meantime, he would gladly continue being both a mother and a father to his kids.

Madison sat at her desk typing a review that was overdue. She had a good excuse for being late, though, as she also had to get out her column and two other reviews for an upcoming double issue.

She doubted that anyone there would be sympathetic, least of all Giselle, since everyone had to carry their weight right now.

Can't complain, since that's why I took the job, she thought, finishing up the piece. Could she help it if she suddenly had more to think about than work ever since she had gone to the jazz club with Stuart? If nothing else, it convinced her that there was more to life than work.

"Busy…?" the deep voice said.

Madison looked up and saw Larry Wellington standing there. He was fifty-something and lanky, and he was wearing what looked like a blond toupee. "Just a little," she said. "What's up?"

"It sure isn't this book," he said, placing the hardcover on her desk. "I tried reading it here, at home, even while hanging out at my girlfriend's place. It's just not for me. I don't want to simply give it a major thumbsdown, so I thought you might want to switch books to at least give this one a fighting chance. What do they say? Different strokes for different folks?"

She gazed at the science fiction title. Not exactly her

cup of tea, but she figured she might need a favor from him sometime. "No problem. I have a few unread books in a pile over there. Take your pick."

He grinned. "Thank you, I'll do that."

"Just remember, you owe me."

"I won't forget," he promised.

Madison smiled and got back to work as he left. Just then, a thought entered her head that she knew she had to act on before she lost her nerve. She would invite Stuart to dinner—she figured she owed him one after their great jazz date.

When his cell phone rang, Stuart was sitting in the living room watching a DVD with the girls. He enjoyed this time as one of the best bonding experiences they had.

His eyes lit, though, when he saw the caller was Madison.

He stood and went to another room so he wouldn't disturb Dottie and Carrie, who were locked into the animated movie.

"Hey," he said.

"Hello."

"Nice to hear from you."

"But yet you haven't called me," she noted.

That caught Stuart off guard. "I've been meaning to, but—"

"I'm just playing with you," Madison assured him. "You've got a lot on your plate."

"We all do," he told her, feeling a little guilty.

"Very true. Anyway, since I really enjoyed listening to Chad sing, I wanted to return the favor."

"You want to go hear him again?" Stuart asked.

"Actually, I was hoping I could cook you dinner," she said. "It's probably short notice for today, but how about tomorrow?"

"Tomorrow is good," he responded. "I'd love to have dinner with you."

"Does six work for you? Or is that too early?"

"Six is perfect. Shall I bring the wine?"

"Sure," Madison said enthusiastically.

Madison paused, then said, "You can bring your girls, too, if you want…"

Stuart paused to think. He wasn't sure it was a good idea to introduce his kids to any women before he knew where it was going, if anywhere. He had to protect them from getting hurt as best he could.

"Thanks, but it's probably best if they sit this one out," he responded. "Hope you understand."

"I do," Madison said. "I just didn't want you to think I was ignoring them."

"I didn't," Stuart promised. "I appreciate the thought."

"Well, I won't keep you. I'll see you tomorrow at six. And bring your appetite."

He chuckled. "I will."

After disconnecting, Stuart phoned Grace, hoping she was available to watch the girls.

"I have some studying to do, but I can bring my

books over there and keep the girls company at the same time," Grace told him.

"I'll make it worth your while," Stuart said. He realized he was imposing on her busy school life.

"Don't worry about it," Grace said. "I like hanging out with Carrie and Dottie."

"Well the feeling is mutual."

Stuart thanked Grace again. He looked forward to seeing what kind of cook Madison was. Something told him he wouldn't be disappointed.

"Daddy's going on a date," Carrie giggled as Stuart did some last-second prepping.

"Who with?" Dottie asked.

What do I tell them that won't bring up a lot more questions? Questions that I don't have answers for? he thought. "She's an old friend of your Aunt Holly's."

Carrie lifted a thin brow. "Do you like her a lot?"

"Right now I like her as a friend," Stuart said uneasily. He certainly wasn't about to get their hopes up prematurely that he might actually have found someone to build a future with.

"Are you bringing her here so we can meet her?" Dottie questioned.

"Not today, but maybe in the future," he said waveringly. "Would that be all right with both of you?"

"Yeah, I think so," Dottie said, twisting her lips.

"Me, too," Carrie said.

Stuart smiled slightly. "We'll have to work on that.

I'm sure she'd be happy to meet Holly's sweeter-than-honey nieces."

They giggled.

"Is she as pretty as Aunt Holly?" asked Dottie.

"I believe she is," Stuart said, slipping into his blazer. "But not half as pretty as my little angels."

They ate that up as he expected and followed him downstairs like puppies into the gourmet kitchen, where Grace was baking cookies.

"I'll leave you two in Grace's capable hands," he said. "And save some of those cookies for tomorrow."

"We will," Dottie said.

"If you need anything—" he said to Grace.

"Don't worry, we'll be fine. Won't we, girls?"

"Of course," Carrie said.

Stuart gave them both a hug and left for his dinner date.

Chapter 8

Madison was a trifle nervous about making dinner for a man for the first time since relocating to Portland. She considered herself a pretty good cook, but had gotten out of the practice of making fancier food.

I definitely don't want to embarrass myself, she thought. *Or have Stuart put off by a terrible meal.*

Not that he seemed like the type of man who would judge a woman's worth solely on her culinary skills. On the other hand, Madison believed that since he was the father of two girls, any woman in his life should at the very least be able to feed them properly.

She knew she wasn't exactly in his life in that way, and maybe never would be. But she wasn't opposed to seeing how far things could go with them. Assuming he felt the same way.

Madison checked the food one last time. The meal would be breaded pork chops, seasoned brown rice, homemade biscuits and steamed carrots. For dessert, she had used an old recipe for peach cobbler that she'd gotten from her grandmother.

I'm sure Stuart's wine will fit nicely with the dinner, she thought, heading back up the curving stairwell to finish dressing.

Not wanting to overdo it or underwhelm him, she settled on an orange scoop-neck top and a black pencil skirt, which were both figure-flattering. She slipped into a pair of wedge sandals. She wore her hair up, accentuating her cheekbones, and added sterling silver earrings and a matching necklace to complete the outfit. After a quick spray of fragrance, Madison was all set.

She heard a car drive up, and a peek out the wooden blinds confirmed it was Stuart. Madison tried to suppress the butterflies in her stomach. She wanted to enjoy the evening and not let her nervousness ruin their dinner date.

"This bottle of Pinot gris is from a local vineyard," Stuart said, handing it to Madison, who looked as lovely as ever. "I know the owner personally."

"Impressive," she said. *But not quite as impressive as you.* He was smartly dressed and looked good enough to eat. She blushed at the thought. "I'm sure it's tasty."

"There's only one way to find out...." Stuart took the bottle from her and headed to the kitchen. In the process, he took a sweeping glance of the roomy town house, from its exposed brick to wood beams to hard-wood flooring. "Nice place you have here," he told her.

"I'm pretty comfortable with it," Madison said.

"You should be. Somehow it suits you."

"I think you're right, it does." She liked how he took charge with the wine, opening it while she got out two goblets.

Stuart poured a small amount in the glasses. "See what you think."

Madison tasted it, allowing it to swirl around in her mouth. "It's wonderful," she said with a smile.

He smiled, too. "Glad you like it."

She met his eyes. "Did you think I wouldn't?"

"No," he had to admit. "But the proof is in the pudding, as they say."

Madison agreed and tasted more of the wine.

"Speaking of pudding, something smells good in here," Stuart said, sniffing. "Apart from you."

"Thank you on both counts." She blushed. "The food's ready to be served. Why don't you make yourself comfortable at the dining room table?"

"Can I help with anything?" he asked.

You're helping a lot by just being here, she thought. "I've got it covered," Madison said, then decided to make him feel useful. "Oh, you can bring the wine and goblets to the table."

Stuart grinned. "Will do." He admired her at work; she was clearly in her element as the woman of the house. Not to mention she was sexy as hell in that outfit.

Five minutes later, they were eating.

Madison waited till Stuart had sampled everything before getting his verdict on the meal. "I hope my cooking agrees with you."

"Does it ever," he said as he sliced through the tender pork chop. "Everything is delicious."

She took a small breath in relief. "I hoped it would be."

"You can cook for me anytime," Stuart said. "I haven't had a home-cooked meal made by someone other than myself in quite a while, so I'm really savoring it."

Madison chuckled lightly. Was he inviting her to cook for him more often? As a good friend, or something more?

"I'll keep that in mind," she told him, and bit into a biscuit. "Are you a good cook?"

"You pretty much have to be when you've got hungry kids to feed. Of course, they frequently talk me into ordering pizza or eating out."

Madison giggled. "I imagine if it were up to them, if your girls are like most kids, they would prefer to eat nothing but junk food."

"You've got that right." Stuart laughed as he scooped up some brown rice. "I do the best I can to make sure they've got some balance in their diet, but it's not always easy as a single dad."

"I'm sure," she said. "So who watches the girls when you're not around?"

"They have a nanny named Grace who does a great job with them."

"But she still can't quite take the place of their mother…"

Stuart sipped his wine and wondered if this was an appropriate subject to talk about. He certainly did not want her to think that he was still pining for his ex-wife.

"I'm not really sure their mother's place is one that should be held on to by them or me. Given that Fawn, my ex, left of her own free will, she gave up any right to have her presence missed." He sighed. "At the same time, I don't want my girls becoming too attached to a college student who, for all her skills at child care, won't be around forever."

Madison understood what he was saying. He wanted someone who would be more permanent in their lives that the girls could get used to. But what did he want for himself? Did he want anyone for a short- or long-term romance?

"Children are pretty resilient," she said. "I suspect that, even if it might be difficult at the time, they would get over losing their nanny, especially if there was an adequate replacement who would stick around for the long haul."

"I'm sure you're right." Stuart drank more wine. He wondered if she had ever thought about having kids. Or if she'd ever considered the possibility of stepping into a ready-made family. "Guess I'll just have to cross that bridge when I get to it."

"Does that bridge include having someone in your life that your girls could get to know?" Madison was shocked that she was being so bold. Would he think she was being too forward? Or would he realize that it was just an honest question?

"I would never rule that out," he told her. "I'm open to that if it happens."

Madison took some comfort in his words, even if they were still just feeling out each other. She noticed that his plate was empty. "Would you like seconds?" she asked. "Or shall I bring in dessert?"

"I'd love seconds," he said, "but my waistline probably wouldn't. So I'll move on to dessert."

She stood while clearing away some things from the table. "Peach cobbler coming right up."

Stuart was enjoying the dessert as much as the food. "You must have been a chef in another lifetime," he said.

"I don't think so," Madison said as she watched him devour the peach cobbler. "But I'm glad you're enjoying it anyway."

Stuart dabbed a napkin at his mouth while wondering if there was anything she wasn't good at. He suspected there wasn't much, which made her all the more appealing.

Yet he still found himself wanting to know more about her.

"Tell me about your family," he said, meeting her eyes.

Madison took a breath, realizing she had him at a disadvantage as she knew about his family in Houston. "I have a sister, Bianca, who is two years older than me. She lives in Las Vegas where she's a reporter."

"How about your parents?"

"They're divorced," she said. "My mom lives in Galveston and my Dad lives in Biloxi, Mississippi."

"Are you close to them?" Stuart asked.

"I'm closest to my sister, though it wasn't always that way. Our family was not really the lovey-dovey type."

"Sorry to hear that."

"So am I," Madison told him, "but that's just the way it was. I'm still in touch with my parents and we all try as best we can to keep the peace."

"I haven't always been as close to my dad as I'd like to be," Stuart admitted. "He had his ideas of what I should do with my life and I had mine. Once my mother passed away, things went from bad to worse for a while, but it seems to have toned down now."

Madison blinked. "He didn't encourage your writing?"

"Not really. Early on, I think he saw writing professionally as another term for unemployment. But as I gained more and more respect, not to mention money, he seems to finally be coming to terms with the fact that I made a smart decision by following this particular dream."

"Has he supported Holly and her dreams?" she wondered.

"Yeah, for the most part," Stuart said. "It seems like she could do no wrong in his eyes. But I'm happy for her. She deserves his love and respect."

"So do you," Madison said, lifting her glass.

"I could say the same thing about your parents," he said. "Guess all we can do is let them come around in their own time and just try to play nice in the mean-time."

She laughed. "That's a good way to look at it."

Stuart decided to change the subject. "So what's the best book you've ever read?"

Madison cocked a brow, wondering if it was a test.

"And don't even think about saying any of my books," he added smartly. "I'm sure there are a ton of books better than mine."

"That's a tough one," she admitted. "I guess I would say *Rebecca* by Daphne du Maurier."

"Good choice," Stuart said, finishing off the peach cobbler.

Madison decided to throw the question back at him. "How about you?"

"I would have to say *Far from the Madding Crowd* by Thomas Hardy."

She smiled. "I would have thought you would pick something in the mystery or thriller genres."

He grinned at her. "I've always been a sucker for the classics, though I also love hard-boiled detective novels."

"Guess there's a lot more for me to learn about you," she said.

"And vice versa," he told her. "Gives us something to look forward to."

"I agree." She smiled, then noticed his dessert plate was empty. "More peach cobbler?"

"Maybe I can take a piece home with me."

"We can do better than that," she suggested. "You can take some home for your daughters."

Stuart smiled at her thoughtfulness. "Thank you. They would love it."

"Good." She looked at him. "Why don't we take our wine into the living room? I'll clean the table later."

"Sounds like a good idea." He welcomed the chance to be closer to her. Clearly, she felt the same way about him. So why not step it up a notch?

They sat on the sofa and Madison immediately felt comfortable with Stuart. He was quite handsome and seemed interested in her. How could she not feel the same way?

"What are you thinking?" Stuart peered into her eyes while holding the goblet, his thoughts working overtime, trying to process that he was there with this gorgeous woman.

"That I'd love to kiss you," she said. Had she really just said that to him? Where did that courage come from?

"Then do it," he told her, taking her wineglass and setting it on the coffee table beside his. "Or, better yet, let me kiss you...."

Stuart tilted his face and moved in to her waiting lips. They parted slightly as he kissed her. Her lips were soft and tender, just as he liked them. He wrapped his arms around the small of her back and drew them even closer while continuing the sweet kiss.

Madison caught her breath as her lips locked with

Stuart's in a full-blown, openmouthed kiss. She couldn't remember ever being so into a kiss.

They went at it for some time, and Madison had become totally lost in the kissing when Stuart slowly pulled back.

"That was some kiss," he said.

She sighed. "Yes, it was."

"If I had known you were such a great kisser, I might have tried that before now."

Madison's lips curved upward. "Had I known the same thing about you, I might have let you."

Stuart chuckled. "Well, as they say, there's no time like the present."

He leaned forward to pick up where they left off, giving Madison a quick peck before she dove into his mouth and all but took control of the kiss.

Enjoying the feel of a man's lips on hers—especially this man's lips—Madison was unabashed about putting her all into the kiss. A tingle between her legs left her wanting for more.

She wondered if Stuart felt the same. Did he crave her every bit as much?

Stuart removed his lips from Madison's mouth and said reluctantly, "I should probably go. The girls will be waiting for me."

Madison swallowed her displeasure, realizing he had obligations that could not be ignored. "All right."

Stuart got to his feet. "Thank you for a lovely dinner."

"Thank you for coming," she said as she stood.

"I wouldn't have missed this opportunity to get to know you better."

She smiled at the thought. "I'll wrap up that peach cobbler for you and your daughters before you go."

Stuart watched her walk away, resisting the urge to follow her and resume their kissing. He hoped he would be able to return the favor one of these days and invite her over. But not until he was sure the girls would fully embrace the idea of him seeing someone.

"Here you go," Madison said, handing him the cobbler.

"Thanks." He stared into her eyes. "I'll call you...."

"I look forward to that," she told him.

Stuart kissed her once lightly on the mouth. "See you later."

As he walked to his car, Stuart came to terms with one simple fact. He liked Madison and wanted to make this work. And he believed she also wanted them to explore this connection. They had to see it through, wherever it might take them.

Chapter 9

Madison could still feel Stuart's tender lips on hers as she drifted off to sleep that night. She hadn't expected the kiss to linger, in spite of its potency. Did that mean she was falling for him?

I guess I'll just have to discover that over time, she thought. Her instincts told her there was something there that Stuart's kiss had unleashed.

But she wouldn't rush it, as she didn't want to jeopardize their potential and the opportunity to get to know his little girls. And Madison wanted to be sure she was in this for all the right reasons—although she couldn't deny that she was attracted to Stuart Kendall, plain and simple. Was that enough?

The next morning, she went jogging with Jacinta. She told her about the fun dinner she'd had with Stuart.

"So things are heating up between you two after all," Jacinta said.

Madison blushed. "Looks that way."

"Why am I not surprised? From what I could see, sexual chemistry practically dripped from you both."

Madison chuckled. "Well, it wasn't quite that extreme. He is an excellent kisser, though."

"Again, I would expect as much," Jacinta said, wiping her brow. "How was he as a lover?"

"I can't speak for that," Madison said. "We haven't gone there yet."

"Nothing wrong with taking your time, girl. I'm sure it'll be well worth the wait."

I'm sure of that, too, Madison thought. An image suddenly flashed in her head of her making love with Stuart. She quickly erased the picture, realizing this wasn't the time or place.

"We'll see what happens," she said. "I'm not looking too far ahead."

"As long as you don't look too far behind," Jacinta warned.

Madison furrowed her brow. "If you're referring to Anderson, I'm definitely not looking in that direction anymore. I'm completely over him."

"That's good to know, because I doubt he has anything on Stuart Kendall."

"Believe me, he doesn't," Madison assured her as they crossed a street.

"Have you met Stuart's kids?" Jacinta asked.

"No, not yet." Madison was aware that Stuart was

very protective of his girls. And he should be after the stunt their mother had pulled. She knew he didn't want to see them go through anything like that ever again. And neither did she.

"I'm sure it'll happen in due time," Jacinta said. "Men like it when women like their children. If he wants to be with you, he'll make sure you have adequate time to get to know his girls."

"I hope so," Madison admitted, sucking in a deep breath and exhaling. She hadn't been around children very much but was hopeful that the girls would like her.

And it was likely she would be just as smitten with them.

Stuart watched the dance recital as Dottie and Carrie moved gracefully alongside the other girls. It reminded him of Holly when she was young, as she'd also been a dancer. He didn't doubt that his daughters were having just as much fun.

"Are those your daughters?" an elderly woman next to him asked.

"Yes, they are," Stuart said proudly, as the two girls danced side by side.

"They're lovely," she gushed.

"Thanks." He smiled broadly at her. "I couldn't be more proud of them."

"Yes, I can see it in your face." She smiled back. "That's my granddaughter over there with the mounds of blond hair."

Stuart gazed at the girl who seemed full of energy. "She's adorable."

"I'm just as proud of her."

"As you should be," he said, again eyeing Dottie and Carrie. He suddenly found himself wishing that Madison was here to see them perform. She certainly seemed interested in meeting the girls, and they had expressed the same interest in meeting her. But he didn't want to get too ahead of himself yet. Even though there seemed to be lots of potential with him and Madison, he still needed to have a better feel for where this was going before he introduced her to his kids.

When the performance ended, the girls raced over to him, all smiles. Stuart gave them both a big hug.

"Did you enjoy it, Daddy?" Dottie asked eagerly.

"How could I not?" he responded, grinning. "You two were amazing."

"You really think so?" asked Carrie.

Stuart touched the tip of her nose. "I *know* so."

"Do you think Mommy would have enjoyed it?"

He cocked a brow, wondering where that had come from. The girls almost never mentioned their mother these days and he didn't encourage them to, all things considered.

"I'm sure she would have," he replied. "But she chose not to be a part of our lives and we have to accept that."

"I know, but it would still be nice if she was here like other moms," Carrie said sadly.

"Maybe you should have brought Aunt Holly's friend," Dottie said, looking up at him.

"You're right," he acknowledged. He preferred that over any talk about Fawn. "Maybe next time."

"Cool," she said.

"Yeah," Carrie agreed. "Or Grace could come."

Stuart smiled, realizing the girls were searching for direction. They needed a reliable female in their lives to support them. Grace, for all her worth, had her own life and could only be there when her schedule permitted. Was it possible that Madison could fill the role of substitute mom someday?

Two days later, Madison was at work on her column. She was trying to focus, but her mind kept coming back to Stuart. She hadn't heard from him since dinner that night. When would he call? Should she make the first move?

No need to stress about this, she told herself. *It's only been a few days.* Why rush a potentially good thing?

She had experienced firsthand what pouring all her emotions into a relationship could do. She didn't want to go there anymore. Especially since, in this case, she wasn't even sure she and Stuart were in a relationship. Madison's cell phone rang. It was her sister.

"Hi there," Madison said.

"How's Portland treating you these days?" Bianca asked.

"It's getting better all the time," Madison said.

"Really? Does that mean you've been asked out?"

"Not necessarily…."

"But that's not a 'no' either," Bianca said. "So who's the lucky man?"

"No one's gotten lucky yet," Madison emphasized, "but I did cook dinner for a man."

"I knew it!" Bianca laughed. "Details…"

"There aren't many at the moment." She paused. "Actually, it was Holly's brother, Stuart."

"Hmm…the same one you were trying to avoid?"

Madison grimaced. "I never said that."

"That's not how I remember it…." Bianca said. "So what about the awkwardness with the Holly drama and all?"

"That's over and done with," Madison said. "I'm cool with Holly now." Even if they might never again be best friends, she respected Holly and wanted only the best for her.

"Well, that's good to know." Bianca took a breath. "So, you're interested in her brother now?"

"I think we're interested in each other."

"Well, that's a start and more than I can say about myself at the moment. There's not much happening for me right now in the dating scene."

Madison had never known her sister to go long without a man in her life. But quality was much better than quantity, and she hoped Bianca held out till she found someone who would really treat her right.

It was advice Madison could just as easily apply to

herself. She wondered if Stuart would prove to be that man who would treat her right for the long haul.

For the time being, she would settle for another date, if it was meant to be.

That evening, Stuart met Chad for a drink at a tavern in the Pearl District.

"So what's got you so tense?" Chad asked over his scotch. "Let me guess, it's got to be a woman, right?"

"You got me."

"Actually, I think she's got you." Chad looked at him. "I assume we're talking about Madison."

"You assumed right." Stuart tasted his rum and coke. "I like her."

"I could see that as plain as day at the club the other night. Tell me something I don't know."

"All right…." Stuart said. "I just want to go into this with my eyes wide open. I'm a single dad whose wife left him for another man, and she's a single woman who may still be trying to overcome an engagement that went nowhere."

"So what is the problem?" Chad asked, a brow raised. "Neither of you are defined by past relationships. We all have them, but we live in the present. Forget about Fawn and her selfishness, just as I'm sure Madison is trying to forget about her ex. If you two hit it off, give it a chance before looking for excuses to go your separate ways."

"You're right," Stuart said. "I think I just needed a fresh perspective. Guess I'm being overly cautious with the girls since they're at the age where they're vulnerable—"

Chad scoffed. "They're not that vulnerable. Kids understand more than you think. I think they get that parents do not always work out and that other people can enter the picture. If you like Madison, I'm sure Carrie and Dottie will cozy up to her in a hurry."

"Maybe so," Stuart said, sipping his drink. "I always want to do right by them."

"And you've done right by them as the ideal dad," Chad said. "Now it's time you do right by yourself, too. I'd say Madison is a very nice step in the right direction."

Chapter 10

"I was wondering if you'd like to check out a movie tonight," Stuart said to Madison after he had dialed her through an iPad video chat.

She looked at his handsome face and didn't have to think about it long. "I'd love to see a movie with you."

He smiled. "Anything in particular you've been waiting to see?"

Madison thought about it. "Nothing in particular, but I am a sucker for romantic comedies."

"So am I," he said. "Can I pick you up at six?" Stuart asked.

"Six is good." Madison gazed at him. "What about your daughters?"

"They're having a sleepover at a friend's house," he said happily.

"Sounds like fun." She remembered doing the same thing with her childhood friends. But she also liked the idea of having the evening to themselves.

"I'll see you then," Stuart said.

After disconnecting, she immediately called Jacinta on her cell phone. "Hey there. I'm going to have to re-schedule our trip to the mall. I've got a movie date to-night with Stuart."

"How nice, and that's totally understandable," Jacinta said. "We can shop anytime."

"Maybe next week?"

"Sure, next week will work. Hope you enjoy the movie, assuming you can take your eyes off each other."

Madison smiled. "You're such a romantic."

"Guilty as charged," Jacinta said. "Now I just have to latch on to a devilishly handsome, well-educated, successful man that I'll actually want to make out with at a movie theater."

Madison chuckled. "I'm sure it will happen soon."

"Not soon enough, girlfriend. But hey, with things moving along for you, it's giving me inspiration."

"Well, it's just a movie."

"It's never just a movie when you're in the company of a single man who's obviously into you."

Madison wasn't sure how to respond to that. She was just as into Stuart, but she was smart enough to know that it still didn't mean they were about to become an item. That would only happen if they were both will-ing to fully put themselves out there.

"I think I'll know a little more about where things are headed soon," she said.

"I'd better let you go, then, and get ready for your date."

"Talk to you later," Madison said.

She freshened up and changed from lounging attire to something appropriate for a movie date.

The movie was funny and romantic with lots of sexual chemistry between the lead actors, but truthfully, Stuart was more attuned to Madison. He put his arm around her and she rested her head against his shoulder, and Stuart enjoyed just how good it felt.

Madison almost felt as if she could fall asleep on Stuart's firm shoulder. Instead, she shared popcorn with him and did her best to get through the movie, though she wished they were in a more intimate setting.

Don't wish for more than you should, she told herself. *Take each step as it comes.*

She believed that Stuart also did not wish to push things too quickly. Not when they obviously enjoyed each other's company and there seemed to be plenty of potential for moving forward.

When the movie ended, Stuart drove Madison home. He wondered if she would invite him in. Or should he not get his hopes up that she was ready for more?

"I'm glad we saw the movie," he told her, glancing her way as they got closer to her home.

"So am I," she responded, smiling. "I don't go often enough."

"Neither do I—at least not to grown-up movies. I try to go whenever I can with the girls."

"But it's not quite the same?"

He chuckled. "Not quite."

"Whenever you want to see a grown-up movie again, let me know."

"I will," Stuart said. "Same with you."

Stuart parked the car in her driveway and walked Madison to the door.

She didn't want to see him leave just yet. "Do you want to come in for a cup of coffee or tea?"

"I'd love to," he said eagerly.

Madison unlocked the door and they went inside. She turned on the light and faced Stuart. Unable to resist, she stepped closer to caress his cheeks and then kiss his mouth, letting her lips linger on his for a long moment. Her body was on fire and she suspected that only he could extinguish the flames.

"Maybe we should forget about the coffee or tea," she whispered through his lips as the kiss continued.

"Maybe we should." His libido was working overtime as he slipped his tongue inside her mouth and held her firmly.

Madison rolled her hands around Stuart's back as his chest brushed against hers, causing her nipples to tingle like crazy. She wanted this man, right now, and had little doubt that he wanted her just as much, feeling the bulge in his pants that was dying to get out.

She broke free of the powerful kiss and gazed hungrily into his eyes. "Do you have protection?"

"Yeah," he said, reaching in his pants pocket to retrieve it. He'd anticipated that something could happen.

Listening to what her body craved, Madison began unbuttoning his shirt and practically ripping it off his broad shoulders before kissing him again ravenously. She stepped back and pulled her top over her head, flinging it away. She waited for Stuart to take off her bra. He did so slowly, then he admired her small, rounded breasts as if they were a work of art. They removed the rest of their clothing and shoes till both were stark naked.

Madison stared in awe at Stuart's fully erect penis, sending a fresh wave of yearning shooting through her. She felt a tad embarrassed, but her unbridled lust to be with him overcame it. She tilted her face and reached once more for his mouth. Stuart delivered, giving her the most passionate kiss yet and causing the temperature to rise in the room.

Stuart, bursting with needs this woman had brought to life, backed her up to the sofa even as their mouths never parted, gently laying her down. He wanted her more than he had ever wanted anyone. He tore open the condom packet and slipped it across his erection.

He looked down at Madison, her eyes hungry for him and her long, lean legs splayed invitingly. Falling on his knees, Stuart placed his face between her legs, wanting to taste her sweetness and increase her longing for him even more. He found her bud, ripe for his mouth and tongue, and went to work.

Madison was overwhelmed by the sheer pleasure

he was giving her. Shamelessly, she took his head and held it in place as an orgasm ripped through her almost immediately.

She gasped, a prisoner to the moment and the man. "Make love to me," she ordered. She needed the feel of him inside her more than anything.

Stuart lifted his face, more than ready to heed to her demand. Nestling himself between her thighs, he entered Madison. She was wet and tight, and the combination sent him into a tizzy as they began to make love.

Madison's breasts heaved as she met Stuart's powerful thrusts halfway, pulling him deeper and deeper inside her. She cried out as he hit the spot again and again.

Desperate for his mouth on hers, she brought his face down and they kissed while their bodies pressed together.

When her climax came, Madison practically elevated off the sofa with her legs wrapped tightly around Stuart's buttocks. He had ignited every fiber in her until her breathing quickened and turned into moans of ecstasy.

Stuart felt the trembling of Madison's moist and supple body, and her sounds of pleasure were music to his ears. Having held back as long as he could, there was no stopping him now in joining her in the throngs of satisfaction.

He burrowed deeper inside her as their slickened bodies stayed in total sync while unleashing his sexual pleasure. A grunt left his mouth and Stuart quavered wildly during the moment of release.

Madison held on to him for dear life as they both

rode the wave of passion together, soaking up each and every second of their first time together.

When it was over, she was thoroughly exhausted but felt more satisfied than she could ever remember after sex.

"Wow...." the word slipped out while Stuart was still halfway on top of her.

"Wow, indeed," he said, squeezing one of her breasts while inhaling the intoxicating scent of their sex. "I'll take that over coffee any day of the week."

"Are you sure you can keep up that type of performance?" she teased.

"I'm sure." Stuart lifted on an elbow and kissed her shoulder. "Especially if it's you I can perform with."

"Sounds perfect." He had instilled in her a desire that she didn't see going away anytime soon.

He grinned, taking her response as a sign that the connection was real. "We're definitely on the same page."

Madison couldn't help but wonder what this meant for their future. Or should she not look too far ahead?

When Stuart suddenly kissed her again, she turned her attention to the here and now, opening her mouth to embrace his fully.

Chapter 11

Stuart peeked in on the girls, who were both in Dottie's room. They were on the bed playing a game, unaware of his presence. He loved the fact that they were so close, virtually inseparable, even though they had their own rooms and had been given space to grow up independently. He did worry a little that they might not be able to cope as well when they eventually would have to live apart. But overall, he was sure it was a good thing that they were here for each other, no matter what came their way in the years ahead.

He smiled as he gazed at his little darlings before quietly slipping away and down the hall. Glancing into the master bedroom, Stuart felt a snippet of desire as he imagined making love to Madison in his king bed. It had been two days since their mutual attraction gave way to unbridled passions. She made him feel good about himself, and he hadn't had a woman do that in a long time.

But was he ready to take her in his own bed? With his kids down the hall?

Would they see her as his girlfriend or as someone who could assume the role of mother in their lives?

Stuart pushed aside his thoughts for now, content to take things one day at a time.

He went downstairs to his study and phoned his editor, Malcolm Warner.

"Thanks for returning my call," Malcolm said.

"Always nice to talk with you," said Stuart.

"I've looked over your novel, and I have to say that it just might be your best one yet."

Stuart grinned. "You really think so?"

"You know me, I never sugarcoat anything," Malcolm insisted. "It's a damned good novel you've got here. I love how you mix the suspense, thrills and romance so seamlessly, and you did it well here."

"That's always the plan," Stuart told him. "Sometimes it works a little better than others."

"Well, trust me when I tell you that it works great in this novel. I really believe you've outdone yourself."

"I appreciate hearing that," Stuart said.

"By the way," Malcolm said, "I loved that piece on you last month in your local magazine."

"Thanks. It was a great interview."

"Maybe the interviewer will do it again just before this novel comes out?" Malcolm suggested.

"I'll work on that," Stuart told him. He suspected that Madison and her boss would welcome another collaboration. For his part, he was more interested in continuing to see Madison on a nonprofessional basis.

Madison didn't exactly have to drag Jacinta to the mall on Saturday. Especially when she'd told her that Stuart would be there signing copies of his last two novels. Madison wanted to go not only because she was dating him, but to show support for his work.

"Are you sure he won't mind if I bring along some of my old books to sign?" Jacinta asked, adding, "I still plan to buy his newest book."

"Stuart will be happy to sign all your books," Madison assured her. "He takes his fan base seriously."

"And we take him just as seriously. The man can flat-out write!"

"You'll get no arguments from me there," Madison said as they approached the bookstore.

"Didn't think so." Jacinta winked at her. "Not when you've got the *ins* with him."

"Those *ins* can only take me so far," Madison said. She thought about how she had yet to be invited into his home. She believed it would happen sooner or later, but for now, she could only wait for Stuart to open up in that respect.

"Who knows how far those *ins* might get you in the long run, girlfriend." Jacinta batted her eyes teasingly. "I'm just saying…"

"Well, say no more," Madison told her as they entered the store. "Let's just see what happens."

Jacinta had practically already forgotten the conversation as she surged ahead to stand in line to get an autographed book.

Madison caught up to her. Though she suspected that Stuart had spotted her, she decided to stay with Jacinta in line rather than cutting to the front to see him.

Feeling tired from signing books, Stuart's face lit up when he saw Madison standing before him. Next to her was a tall, dark-skinned woman with braided hair in a ponytail.

"Hey, Mr. Author," Madison said, smiling.

"Hey, you," he responded.

"This is my neighbor, Jacinta Poole."

"Nice to meet you, Jacinta," Stuart said, stretching to shake her hand.

"You, too," she said. "I've been a fan for years, and now I finally get to have my books signed by you, if that's all right."

Stuart smiled at her, then Madison. "Of course. I'm happy to sign whatever you brought with you."

"Thank you," she gushed, and grabbed a new hardcover book off the stack on the table. "I definitely want an autographed copy of your latest book, too."

"Even better." Stuart held his pen. "What would you like me to say?"

Madison watched with pride as he generously wrote

down every word she wanted in each book, much to the chagrin of others waiting their turn.

She tried to imagine what it must be like to be a famous author. What she knew was that Stuart handled it with poise and professionalism. While he seemed to revel in his success, it clearly was not the most important thing in his life.

His daughters took that spot, and rightfully so. Though she would never want to compete with such affection, Madison did wonder if there was enough room in Stuart's heart for her to be the woman in his life. She hoped so, because she enjoyed his companionship and was optimistic about the direction in which their relationship seemed to be headed.

She grabbed a book from the pile, setting it before Stuart. "Sign it," she said, smiling.

"I think I have a few extras at home," he said. "I'm sure one already has your name on it."

"Yes, this one." Her lashes batted playfully. "I can afford to pay for my copy like any other fan."

"If you insist…" Stuart signed the novel, though they both knew that she was anything but just another fan. An image of them making loved flashed across his mind before he came back down to earth. He admired how beautiful she looked in a multicolored peasant top and white skinny pants. "Here you are," he said.

Madison's heart skipped a beat when she read his words in the book—"To a wonderful, gorgeous woman who is now a part of my life—Stuart."

"Thank you for that," she said softly.

"My pleasure," he said, beaming.

Realizing she was hogging his time, Madison said, "See you later. Have fun."

"I *will* see you later." Stuart winked then turned to the next person in line.

That evening, Stuart showed up at Madison's place, after he'd gotten Grace to watch the girls.

"I couldn't wait to see you," he said between kisses as they got naked in Madison's bedroom.

"I couldn't wait for you to see me and for me to see you—all of you," she said.

Stuart removed his boxers and tossed them to the floor. His desire for her was so strong that he could barely keep his hands off her.

Madison was turned on by seeing him completely naked. His erection made her even more desirous, for it told her just how much he craved her. She would not disappoint.

She pushed him down on the bed and climbed on top of him. Straddling him, she leaned down, kissed his rock-hard chest, and then moved to his mouth where she peppered his lips with hot kisses.

"You're killing me," Stuart said, finding it hard to contain himself and the need to be inside her.

"Don't die yet," Madison teased him. "Not when there's much better things to do...."

She put her open mouth on his again, turning up the heat with a passionate kiss before ending the torture for them both by lowering herself onto his manhood. She felt him throbbing inside her core as she moved fluidly up and down him.

She moaned as he gently rubbed her nipples and pushed himself deeper inside her, bringing their pleasure to new heights. Gripping the headboard for support, Madison was beside herself as she contracted around Stuart's erection, stimulating her to no end. She brought her face down to his and enveloped his lips with hers, tasting, teasing and tantalizing as they kissed with fervor.

"Oh…Stuart," Madison murmured while her orgasm took center stage. Her breath quickened when she reached the apex of utter appeasement, after which she fell onto him, fully expecting him to take over in completing the passion.

Stuart did not disappoint. Easily flipping them over while still wedged inside her, he wrapped her legs up high around his back and made love to her like a man possessed by the woman beneath him.

"You're mine, all mine," he said in a husky voice.

"I am," she said breathlessly. "Make me come again…."

Stuart was determined to do just that, holding back enough to maintain long and even strokes while stimulating her tender spot.

When Madison's body shook violently and she constricted around him, it was the signal he needed to let loose and join her. Spreading her legs wider, Stuart picked up the pace. A guttural wail erupted from his throat with his powerful release.

Even after the moment had passed, they remained locked in coitus while basking in the afterglow.

When Stuart finally climbed off her, all Madison wanted to do was fall asleep in his arms.

Chapter 12

"Hey, sis," Stuart said the next day as he video-chatted with Holly.

"Hey, yourself," she said. "I was just thinking about you."

"Really? What were you thinking about?"

"Last night, Dad and I were looking at family pictures and remembering the good old days when the family was still intact," Holly said, smiling. "Guess I just got a little nostalgic and missed my big brother."

"I'm still here," Stuart said. He was moved by the love she had always shown him. "You know you can call me any time the spirit moves you."

"I know," she said. "And as much as I'd like to more

often, I have to show some restraint and pay attention to my husband."

Stuart laughed. "I understand perfectly." He grinned, thinking this was a perfect time to say what was on his mind. "Speaking of your husband, I've been seeing Madison—"

Holly's eyes popped wide open. "By seeing, do you mean dating?"

"Yes, we're dating," he said. He watched her carefully to gauge her reaction.

"How long has this been going on?"

"Not long," he replied.

"Well, I can't say it's a total shock," she said. "I felt you two would hit it off once you got to know each other."

"Guess you were right," he said. "She's a beautiful woman with lots of character."

"I agree and I'm happy for you both."

"You don't consider any of this kind of weird?" Stuart wondered.

"You mean weird in that I'm married to her ex-fiancé?"

"Yeah."

"Not at all," Holly told him. "People have relationships that don't work out and then they move on. It's a normal part of life. The fact that I happened to fall for Anderson and you for Madison is no big deal. That's just the way it worked out."

"I suppose you're right," he said thoughtfully.

Holly gazed at him. "So is it serious between you two?"

Stuart thought about it. "We haven't made any plans to walk down the aisle or anything, if that's what you're asking."

"It isn't," she said. "I was just wondering what you wanted to come out of this. Or am I asking too many questions?"

He chuckled. "No, you're not." Indeed, he expected as much from her and probably needed it. "I like Madison a lot, but I haven't looked too far down the road yet. I only know that she makes me happy and I want this to work out."

"So do I," Holly said. "Heaven knows you deserve someone who can be true to you and love your daughters the way their mother never did."

Stuart sighed, looking down and then up again. "True."

Holly's eyes narrowed. "You *have* introduced Madison to the girls, right?"

"Uh, no, not yet," he answered.

"Why not?"

Stuart shrugged. "I just want to spare them any unnecessary disappointment in case things don't work out."

"They're not as fragile as you might think," Holly said. "Besides, you can't look at it that way. Believe me, Madison isn't the reincarnation of Fawn. Don't be afraid to take a chance and let her get to know Carrie and Dottie."

"You're right, she's not Fawn," he said, "and I shouldn't allow fear to get the better of me."

"Good! You owe it to them and Madison to see what happens. My guess is that they will all get along splendidly and everything else will take care of itself."

Stuart laughed. "My sister, always thinking positively."

"And just who do you think I inherited that from, big brother?" she asked, grinning.

"Not me," he suggested.

"Of course it was you! You've always done a great job looking at the big picture. And I'm sure you will with this, too, when all is said and done."

Stuart rested on that thought. He liked the idea of moving things up a notch in their relationship.

Madison was surprised when she got a call from Holly. Though they had made their peace, neither had gone out of their way to keep in touch. It was something Madison had been planning to rectify, especially now that she was involved with Stuart.

Freshly showered and still in her bathrobe, Madison sat on the bed and answered her cell phone.

"Hi, Holly," she said guardedly.

"Hey, Madison," Holly said. "I wanted to see how you're doing and say that I hope you're enjoying springtime in Portland. Everything is so green then!"

"Yes, I am enjoying it," Madison said. And she could think of a very good reason for that.

"So, I hear that you and Stuart are dating now," Holly said.

"Yes, we've started seeing each other." Madison was not really surprised that Stuart had told her, knowing they were close. "I never expected it when I moved here. It just happened...."

"Well, I wanted you to know that I think it's a wonderful thing."

"You do?"

"Sure," Holly said. "Stuart seems crazy about you, and I suspect you feel the same about him."

"I do," she admitted. "Your brother is a good man with a good head on his shoulders, and he adores his kids."

"I agree on all counts," Holly said. "Speaking of kids, Stuart told me that you haven't met Dottie and Carrie yet."

"Yeah, I've been wondering about that," Madison said. "I know he's just being overprotective and—"

"And foolish," Holly broke in. "I told him to get over it and do the right thing and let his girlfriend meet his girls."

"How did he react?" Madison asked, eager to know.

"Let's just say the wall he's built around Carrie and Dottie is coming down."

"That's good to know," Madison said.

"He just needed a little nudge in the right direction," Holly said.

Madison smiled. "Thanks for speaking to him on my behalf."

"Hey, that's what friends are for. You would have done the same thing were the situation reversed."

Madison thought about that and believed she would have. After a moment, she asked, "How are things with you and Anderson?"

"They're good," Holly said. "We're good."

"I'm glad." Madison paused. "Listen, I meant what I said the last time we spoke. I'm happy for you guys and want only the best for you."

"I appreciate that," Holly said. "I feel the same way about you and Stuart."

"Thanks. We're still in the early stages of dating, but we do seem to be kindred spirits so…"

"So enjoy what life throws at you and enjoy each moment."

"I intend to," Madison said. They talked a few more minutes before hanging up. She had gained a whole new respect for Holly. But more importantly, she was excited that she might be getting an invitation from Stuart to meet his children.

Stuart was helping the girls with their homework when he brought up the subject of Madison.

"I was thinking about inviting Madison over for dinner on Sunday," he said. "What do you think?"

"You should do it," Carrie declared.

"Yeah?" He looked across the table at her.

"I'm sure," she said.

"You, too?" Stuart asked Dottie.

She nodded. "You didn't have to wait so long, Daddy. We've been dying to see her since your first date."

He smiled. "Is that so?"

Dottie frowned. "We know Mommy isn't coming back."

Stuart met her eyes. "No, she isn't...." he said.

"So you should have someone in your life," Carrie said. "We want you to be happy."

"I'm happy with you two honey bunnies."

"We know you are," Dottie said.

"And if you fall in love with Madison and want to marry her, you should do it," Carrie told him. "It's okay if she becomes our new mom."

His brows rose. "Hey, we're nowhere near that stage yet," he said, though he could imagine their relationship progressing to that level. "Why don't you meet her first and find out if you like her? Then we'll see what the future holds. Even if she only ends up being a good friend, she can still be a part of your lives if you want."

Both girls seemed happy with that possibility. Stuart suspected that what they really wanted was a new mom, as the old one had become a distant memory. He wondered if Madison had any desire to be a mother.

"I'd like you to meet my girls," Stuart told Madison as they lay naked and cuddled in her bed later that week.

"Are you sure?" She looked up at him, not wanting him to do anything he had reservations about.

"Yes, I'm sure," he told her. "It seems like a logical step at this point. They certainly are excited about meeting you."

"I feel the same way about meeting them," Madison said, as she draped her leg across his. "I was beginning to wonder if you felt I wasn't good enough to hang out with your kids."

"It was never about that," Stuart assured her. "I just wanted them to first get used to the idea that I was seeing someone. Then I wanted to feel that this was going somewhere before introducing you to them and having the girls become too attached to you."

Madison tried her best to understand his viewpoint. She supposed that his daughters were vulnerable to attachment at their age, especially after being without a mother in their lives for years now. She wanted to fit into the role of someone who would be there for them, even if this was her first experience with dating a man with children.

She met Stuart's eyes. "So you think this is going somewhere then?"

"Yeah, I think so."

Her lashes fluttered. "And where is that exactly?"

"I think it can go as far as we want to take it," he said.

"I believe that, too," she said.

"We're certainly in sync and that means a lot after being with someone who proved to be totally out of sync with me."

Madison gave him a thoughtful look. "You're singing to the band," she said lightheartedly.

"Guess I am." He grinned. "Anyway, I was thinking

you could come over for dinner Sunday. The girls insist on helping me cook to make it really special."

Madison smiled. "That sounds sweet. I'd love to come for dinner on Sunday."

"Then it's a date." Stuart slid his hand across her leg and between her thighs. "Right now, there are other things we can do to keep ourselves occupied."

She trembled slightly as he stimulated her. "You're insatiable."

"I have you to blame for that," he said, quickly becoming aroused.

Madison loved the thought of turning him on at any time. "In that case, it looks like we'll have to do something about it."

Stuart leaned toward her face and kissed Madison's lips, tasting wine from earlier. "Yes, let's do something about it...."

She put her arms around his neck and began to kiss him passionately as he returned the kiss with equal fervor.

They made love for the second time that evening, cementing in Madison's mind the reality that they were indeed a couple made for each other in the bedroom. And the connection was also there in the way their personalities clicked. Even their professional lives had intersected successfully.

Now she wanted to make inroads with Stuart's family and be a good friend to his girls. Something told

Madison it was doable, which gave her a whole new reason to believe she might have finally found Mr. Right, with his offspring as an added bonus.

Chapter 13

Madison was a tad nervous about meeting Stuart's girls for the first time. Oddly enough, she had nearly met them once in Houston when she lived there, but then had had to go out of town on business. *I'll just be myself and trust that I can win them over,* she thought.

She was dressed casually in a blue top, white capri jeans and moc flats. Madison sucked in a breath and rang the doorbell.

The door opened right away and a thin girl, tall for her age, stood there, smiling. "Hi, you must be Madison."

"I sure am." She smiled back. "And you are…?"

"Dottie."

"Nice to finally meet you, Dottie."

"You, too."

"May I come in?" Madison asked.

"Yeah," Dottie said, giggling.

Inside, Madison was greeted by Stuart, who looked dashing in a gray shirt and black pants. He kissed her on the cheek. "I see you've met Dottie."

"Yes." She grinned at the girl. "And where's…?"

"I'm right here," said a girl as Madison watched her walk out of the kitchen. "I'm Carrie."

"Hi, Carrie." Madison put her hand on the girl's shoulder, noting she had flour on her top. "Looks like you've been busy cooking."

She looked a little embarrassed. "We've all been busy. Hope you like everything we made for you."

"I'm sure I will," Madison said, relieved to have broken the ice.

"Why don't you girls wash up," Stuart said, "while I give Madison the grand tour."

"See you soon," Dottie said, and she and her sister ran toward the stairs.

Stuart waited till they had disappeared from sight before putting his hands on Madison's waist. "So what do you think of my little ones?"

"I think they're beautiful," she said candidly.

"I'm sure they see you the same way," he said. "I certainly do."

Madison blushed. "Thank you for inviting me over."

"Thanks for coming." Stuart couldn't resist giving her a kiss on the lips, even though he suspected his girls might be peeking at them. If so, he did not mind, as he had already made it clear to them that he had grown very fond of Madison and wanted her to be part of their lives, too. So far, it seemed to have gotten off to a good start. He took Madison's hand. "Let me show you around."

Madison had already glimpsed the magnificent two-story Victorian and had been awed by its amazing exterior and impressive grounds. She was equally impressed with the interior architecture that appeared to have original woodwork along with some elegant remodeling.

Each room seemed more impressive than the last with a combination of art deco, contemporary and period furnishings. She loved the girls' bedrooms—both were colorful and apparently outfitted with their individual tastes in mind.

When Madison took a look at Stuart's bedroom, she could see that, though it was charming and well kept with a king-sized platform bed, it still lacked a woman's touch. Maybe she could do something about that if he let her.

"It's fabulous," she told him as they stood in the upstairs hallway.

"Thanks," Stuart said humbly.

"Did you fix it up yourself?"

"I wish. I had an expensive decorator take care of that."

She wondered if it had been before or after his wife had left them. Not that it mattered. As far as Madison was concerned, the past was staying in the past for both of them. "Well, I commend the decorator."

He smiled. "Would you like to freshen up before dinner?"

Madison nodded. "I would."

She was shown to a huge bathroom adjacent to what appeared to be a guest room and told to make herself at home.

Not too surprisingly, she was already starting to do just that.

"This is delicious," Madison said as they sat at the formal dining room table beneath a crystal chandelier.

"You really think so?" Carrie asked eagerly. She had made bran muffins and Dottie had helped make the salad.

"Yes, I do," Madison said. "Looks like we have two little chefs in the making...and one big one."

"Cool," Dottie said with a giggle.

"Yeah, definitely cool," Stuart said. He had prepared the baked chicken and macaroni and cheese himself.

"So you're friends with Aunt Holly?" Carrie said as she ate her salad.

"Yes, I sure am," Madison said.

"And you know Uncle Anderson, too?" Dottie asked.

Madison looked at Stuart, feeling more amused than uneasy by the question. "Yes, I'm friends with him, too."

"Cool," she said, biting into a muffin.

Stuart gave Madison an appreciative nod that she had handled the awkward question with such grace. It told him that she had put the Anderson drama behind her for good, just as he had put the drama with Fawn behind him. He considered it a good sign that they were ready to progress in their relationship without looking back.

"Where do you live?" Carrie asked.

"Not too far away from here."

"May we come over to your house sometime?" Carrie asked.

Madison smiled. "Sure, I'd love that, if it's all right with your father."

Stuart felt all eyes turn on him. "Of course. Any time Madison invites you is fine with me, as long as you've done your homework."

Both girls smiled brightly and Madison sensed the girls' connection as twins.

"I understand that you girls go bike riding with your father," she said.

"Sometimes," Dottie said. "Do you ride, too?"

"Quite a bit, actually," admitted Madison. "Maybe we can go riding together."

"That would be fun," Carrie said.

"Yeah," Dottie agreed.

"Then we'll do it," Madison said. The glint in Stuart's eyes told her they had his wholehearted approval.

Things seemed to be going as well as she could have hoped, and Madison had a feeling that this really was the start of something special.

The next week, Madison took the girls for the day. Though Stuart had expressed concern that they might be too much of a burden on her, she begged to differ. It wasn't as though she had never been around children before. Besides, if she was to become a truly meaningful part of their lives, Madison wanted to gain their trust and prove to Stuart that she embraced this part of his life.

She took Carrie and Dottie shopping, giving them the opportunity to show her what they liked and didn't like in clothing. The girls seemed thrilled by the experience, and they seemed to welcome her participation and the responsibility she was giving.

Afterward, they had hamburgers and fries at a fast-food restaurant.

"Your father tells me that you're both dancers," Madison said, biting into a fry.

"Yeah," Carrie said. "But Dottie's better than I am."

"Really?" Madison looked at Dottie. "Is that true?"

She grinned. "I guess."

"Do you want to be a dancer when you grow up?"

"No," Dottie said, sipping a soft drink. "I want to be a teacher."

"That's a good profession," Madison said. "We certainly need more teachers. What about you, Carrie?"

"I want to be an author like Daddy."

Madison smiled. "That's a good profession, too. Everyone likes to read, so authors have a ready-made audience."

"Do you like working at a magazine?" Carrie asked.

"Yes, I like it very much. My job gives me the freedom to work on my own time. I also enjoy reading books and sharing my thoughts with readers."

"Have you read any of Daddy's books?" Dottie asked.

"How about every single one of them," Madison responded with pride.

"That's great," she said, grinning.

"I think so, too," added Carrie.

"Your father's a terrific writer who brings so much joy to readers around the world," Madison said. "I just happen to be one of them."

She was enjoying this time with Stuart's girls and could tell that they were, too. It was a good way to connect with them.

In the afternoon, Madison took the girls to the Oregon Museum of Science and Industry. Once inside, they went to the planetarium, saw a film in IMAX and checked out the Science Store, much to the girls' delight.

Afterward, Madison took them back to her place for milk and cookies. Carrie and Dottie sat on opposite sides of her on the couch while she read them a children's book.

An hour later, Stuart showed up as scheduled. He gave his girls a hug and Madison a kiss. "Hope they didn't run you ragged."

"Not at all," she assured him. "We had a great time."

"Really?" He looked at the girls, who backed her up on that. "I'm happy to hear it." Not that it was a big surprise. It was obvious that they enjoyed each other's company, something that would be key with anyone he exposed the girls to. Being that it was Madison made it all the more satisfying.

"Do you want to sit down for a while?" Madison asked him.

"Tempting, but I've got some writing to do to stay on schedule, so I'll have to take a rain check." Stuart gazed at the girls. "We'd better get out of Madison's hair now. I'm sure we've taken up enough of her time today."

He watched as the three looked at each other conspiratorially before Dottie said, "We were hoping we could stay overnight...."

"Yeah, Madison said we could," Carrie agreed.

Stuart locked eyes with Madison, figuring she probably was not as keen on the idea as they were.

"I did say that and meant it," she told him evenly. "We've had such fun together. It would be a wonderful way to end our day. Plus, we're not through reading yet."

"What about school tomorrow?"

"Got that covered, too," Madison said with a smile. "I can stop at your house later to get them a fresh set of clothes and drop them off at school myself."

"Are you sure that it wouldn't put you out of your way too much?" Stuart asked. He wasn't used to anyone being so helpful with his daughters, without asking for anything in return.

"Not at all," Madison insisted. "It's on my way to work anyway. Don't worry about it. We'll be fine. Right, girls?"

"Right," they agreed in unison.

"Looks like you've thought of everything," Stuart

said. "And I'm clearly outnumbered three to one. Guess it's settled then."

"Guess it is." Madison gave him a toothy smile and watched the girls high-five each other. They were clearly enjoying a little independence from their father, but they were also happy to spend time with her. She saw this as a win-win for everyone. Especially her, since she saw it as a sign that she was taking another step toward becoming more a part of Stuart's life.

Chapter 14

On Monday, Madison was summoned to Giselle's office. When she got there, her boss was talking on the phone, but Giselle waved her in.

Madison thought about Stuart and the girls while waiting. She'd had so much fun with them yesterday. It made her realize what she had been missing by not having children all these years. Of course, she had not been fortunate enough to find someone who wanted a family and would stick around long enough to show the type of love and commitment she wanted.

Until now. She was sure Stuart was that type of man. But would he want more children? Or was he happy just having Carrie and Dottie?

Madison had to ask herself the same question. Was

she good stepmother material? And could she be happy if she never had any children of her own?

Those questions were put on hold as Giselle got off the phone.

"Sorry to keep you waiting," she said. "That was Beatrice Swain, the bestselling author of—"

"Literary fiction," Madison finished. "I've read all her books."

Giselle smiled. "Well, in that case, you'll love my next assignment for you." She sighed. "Ms. Swain is somewhat of a recluse these days. She lives on the Oregon coast in Lincoln City, which is about a two-hour drive. After much effort, she's consented to her first interview in years. With the wonderful piece you did on Stuart Kendall, I'd like you to go there and talk to Beatrice about her new book and whatever else you can get out of her about her amazing career."

"I'd be honored," Madison said. It was an assignment that she was more than up for, and it would give her the opportunity to visit the coast for the first time.

"I was hoping you'd say that," Giselle said.

"Will John Gregg be accompanying me to take pictures?" Madison asked.

"Actually, we've arranged for a local photographer to take pictures of Ms. Swain," she responded. "I set up the interview for Wednesday at noon."

Madison nodded. "I'll be there."

"I'm sure you'll do a great job."

Madison smiled, appreciating the confidence Giselle

had in her interviewing ability. Now she needed to brush up on her Beatrice Swain books before taking on this task.

"Hey, good-looking," Stuart said, grinning as Madison's face appeared on his cell phone for a video chat early Tuesday.

"Hello, Mr. Handsome," she said in return. "Hope you weren't in the middle of writing a chapter or something...."

"Not at all. I was just chilling after taking the girls to school."

"They are as cute as can be," Madison said. "I'm so happy to get to know them."

"I can assure you the feeling's mutual."

"Good," she said, smiling. "Listen, I'll be going to the coast on Wednesday morning to interview a writer for the magazine. I'd love it if you could come with me for a day trip."

"Count me in," Stuart said. "I'd be delighted to go with you to the coast. Grace should be able to watch the girls for me."

"Perfect." Madison smiled again. "I haven't seen the ocean in quite a while."

"It's definitely a sight to see. I took Dottie and Carrie to the beach last summer and they had a ball."

"You're such a terrific dad," she couldn't help but say.

He grinned. "I have to be, since I'm all they've got. But they give me as much back as I give them."

Madison took a breath. "Do you think you'd ever want any more children?" Okay, she had put it out there, for better or worse.

"Sure, why not?" Stuart responded without pause. "I think the girls would love to have a baby brother or sister, or both, to dote over."

"And how would you feel about it?" she asked.

"Same way. I love children and always envisioned a house full of them. If I ever marry again and my wife wants to add to our family, I'm all for it."

Madison smiled. Stuart always knew all the right words to say. "Just curious," she told him.

"I take it you wouldn't mind having children of your own?" Stuart asked directly.

"That would be nice—one or two—if it happened in the course of a loving relationship."

He nodded. "Wouldn't expect it to be any other way."

"Well, I'd better get back to work," she said.

"Okay. Thanks for the invite to the coast. Should be fun to get away from here for a while with you."

Madison's eyes crinkled as she smiled. "That goes double for me."

When she hung up, Madison couldn't take the smile off her face. It truly did seem like he was the man she'd waited all her life for. She only hoped she didn't suddenly wake up and find this was just a dream.

They arrived in Lincoln City on Wednesday morning. Madison brought Stuart, thinking it would seem more like an informal conversation than an interview.

The interview with Beatrice Swain went smoothly. Madison found her to be a gracious host. Though she was clearly slowing down at seventy-three, the author was still sharp and quick-witted. Madison was able to get Beatrice to talk about her long life and writing career, along with the strengths of her latest literary classic.

But the most entertaining part of the interview was learning that Beatrice was a big fan of Stuart's. The two clicked over tea and chocolate chip cookies, comparing notes and anecdotes. Instead of feeling like the third wheel, Madison was in on every conversation and, in fact, helped the two famous writers feel at ease with each other. The photographer took plenty of pictures.

Afterward, Madison and Stuart went for a walk on the beach, hand in hand. The ocean was calm and the sky a beautiful shade of blue.

"You did a terrific job handling Beatrice," Stuart said, eyeing Madison.

"I think you had a little something to do with that," she told him. "You two had a natural connection."

"Maybe, but not nearly as natural as the one I have with you."

Her face glowed with pleasure as she looked up at him. "You say the sweetest things."

"I mean them," he insisted.

"Well, we do seem to have something special going on here," she conceded, squeezing his hand a little more.

"I'll be honest and say that I wasn't sure I'd ever meet someone who could put the sparkle back in my eyes."

Madison felt a tingle run through her. "I could say the same thing,"

"The girls could see it, too," Stuart said. "They already consider you practically part of the family."

"That's great. And I mean that more than I can say," she said. But would *practically* being part of the family perhaps lead to one day becoming a full-fledged member of the family? "I feel the same way about them."

Stuart let the words ring in his head. "I've always wanted to protect Dottie and Carrie from being put in a bad situation like when their mother left. You've shown me that it's worth it to take a chance and open your heart."

Madison smiled. "I'll try not to disappoint you—or them."

"I doubt that you ever would," he told her, sensing that she was every bit into this relationship and being supportive of his daughters as he was. It was all he ever wanted in a woman. Now he only wanted to hold on to this one.

She stopped walking, feeling light on her feet and blessed to have someone instill such faith in her, not only as a girlfriend but also as a friend to his girls. Lifting her chin, she kissed him and held the kiss as Stuart reciprocated.

Afterward, they gazed out over the ocean, enjoying the moment and each other's company.

Chapter 15

At the Portland International Airport, Madison greeted her sister, Bianca, who had decided on the spur of the moment to come for a visit.

"Let me look at you, girl," Bianca said after they hugged. "You've got some color in your cheeks, so obviously things are looking good for you."

Madison smiled and studied her. Bianca was an inch shorter, the same size and had long, curly blondish-brown hair that looked great on her. "I could say the same about you."

Bianca smiled. "I'm hanging in there, trying to make the most of my life in Vegas."

"Just as I'm trying to do in Portland."

"You can tell me all about that on the way to your place," Bianca said.

Soon they were driving down the interstate.

"So how are things going with you and Stuart?" Bianca asked, looking at Madison.

"Really good," she answered happily.

"You mean good sex, good chemistry and good rapport with his children?"

"All of the above," Madison told her.

"Sounds like a match made in heaven," Bianca said enviously.

"More like a match made in the Rose City," she said.

Bianca chuckled. "Whatever you say. Obviously, moving here turned out to be a good thing for you—in more ways than one."

"I would say so."

"Has anyone said the *L* word yet?"

"If you mean *love,* no," Madison said. "There's no rush."

"But you're feeling it?" Bianca asked.

"Honestly, I hadn't really thought about that," Madison said. "We're just enjoying each other's company right now and letting things play out."

"Sounds like a major case of denial to me."

"Not denying anything," Madison said. "I prefer to let actions speak for themselves."

"And is the action between you and Stuart telling you that he wants you to be together for the long haul?" Bianca asked bluntly.

Madison gave the question some thought as she exited the freeway. She understood that both she and Stuart were treading carefully now in that respect, having opened their hearts deeply in the past only to be burned.

But clearly her feelings toward him were developing into love. Was the same true for him?

"I've certainly been led to believe that Stuart thinks the world of me, and his girls do, too," Madison said. "I think he does see this as a long-term relationship. Right now that's good enough for me."

"So when do I get to meet this man?" Bianca asked anxiously.

"Tonight."

"Oh, good," she said. "I can't wait to see the man who's lit a fire under my little sister."

Madison grinned. "He's just as eager to meet you."

Bianca turned toward her. "How's the situation with his sister working out?"

"Great. We're talking again, and Holly is completely supportive of me dating her brother."

"As she should be, considering that she's now married to your ex," Bianca said.

"Let's not even go there," Madison said as she pulled up into her driveway. "Anderson and I were through a long time ago. I've accepted it and moved on. Just be happy for me."

"I am," Bianca promised. "I've always wanted you to be happy. If that comes from Stuart, more power to him—and you."

Madison smiled. "Let's go inside and I'll give you the grand tour."

Stuart was a little nervous about meeting Madison's sister for the first time. He suspected she would be eyeing him closely to see if he was good enough to be with Madison. Not that he could blame her. He had felt the same way about Anderson being with Holly. It had taken him a while to get used to the idea. But he had, and now he believed she had made the right choice by picking Anderson to spend the rest of her life with.

Just as he believed that Madison might be that woman he could make a life with. She really was every-thing he ever wanted. The fact that she had won Carrie and Dottie's approval meant everything to him. There was a genuine affection between Madison and the girls that he believed would only grow stronger over time.

But at the moment, he was on the hot seat, and he needed to win over Madison's sister.

Stuart got out of his car and headed up the walkway. The door opened before he could ring the bell.

The woman who greeted him bore a strong resem-blance to Madison, save for looking slightly older and having a different hair color and style. "You must be Bianca," he said.

"I am." She smiled. "And you must be Stuart."

"That's me." He stuck out his hand. "Nice to meet you."

She ignored his hand and gave him a quick hug. "You, too."

Madison smiled, watching her sister and boyfriend play nice from the start. She saw this as a good sign that they would get along just fine.

"Hey," she said to Stuart.

"Hey." He tilted his face and planted a kiss on her

mouth. "I didn't realize you and your sister were practically twins."

Madison gave a little laugh. "Not quite Dottie and Carrie, but the likeness has always been there."

"Can't say it's quite the same with me and my sister," Stuart said, "but some people swear the resemblance is strong."

"I can see it," Madison said. "I'm sure Holly can, too."

"Maybe," he said.

"Does anyone want anything to drink?" she asked, looking from Stuart to Bianca and back.

"Wine would be nice," Stuart said.

"Same here," Bianca said.

Madison went to get the wine and some snacks, leaving them alone to size up one another. Knowing her sister, she was sure Bianca would give Stuart the third degree. She had no doubt he could handle himself with whatever she threw at him.

The bottom line was that Stuart was the real deal, and Madison wanted her sister to understand this and support her choice in a man.

Stuart sat down with Bianca, who had checked him out more than once, as if to later give her assessment to Madison. He understood her reaction, given the bond between the two siblings.

"So you're a big-time author, huh?" Bianca asked.

"Not that big," Stuart said, "but, yes, an author."

"I can't say I read all that much, but I'll look you up in the iBookstore and see what's there."

"You should find all of my books there," he was proud to say.

Bianca gazed at him. "Must be challenging to be a single dad with two kids."

"Actually, it's been more rewarding than anything," he said. "They make me whole and make me appreciate what it takes to raise two children who will one day hopefully become productive adults with lives of their own."

"It would be easier if you had some help in that department," she said, eying him.

"I have a nanny who does a terrific job with them," he said. "But, of course, my girls and I would welcome Madison's presence in our lives in whatever capacity she wishes."

"Then you see this as more than just a casual thing?" Bianca asked bluntly.

"Yes, I definitely see my relationship with Madison as much more than that." Stuart met her eyes. "I know your sister has had relationship troubles in the past, but that has nothing to do with the future. Whatever happens with us, we'll make the decisions together."

She smiled. "Okay."

Guess I passed the test thus far, Stuart thought, as Madison returned with a tray of crackers, cheese and nuts, along with three goblets of wine.

"Hope you two have been getting to know each

other," Madison said. Judging by the looks on their faces, she suspected that was in fact the case.

"We sure have," Bianca said, taking her wineglass. "Looks like Stuart is a keeper."

"Glad you feel that way," Madison said as she sat next to him. "I certainly think he's special."

"So are you," Stuart told her. "And, I can see that it runs in the family."

Bianca blushed. "Why, thank you for that." She tasted the wine. "You don't happen to have a cousin or someone who's available and able to relocate to Las Vegas, do you?"

He laughed. "Afraid not, sorry."

"Oh, well, it was worth a try," she said with a shrug.

"I think some lucky gent in Vegas will find you on his own and be damned glad he did," Stuart told her.

"He really is a gem, Madison," Bianca said. "I'll definitely keep my eyes open for such a lucky gent."

"Good idea," Madison told her cheerfully. "That way you won't miss him."

She smiled at Stuart and sipped her wine. Apparently he had won over Bianca. This gave Madison yet another reason to believe that things were starting to finally come together in her life.

Chapter 16

On Memorial Day, Stuart took Madison and the girls over to Lyle Creighton's house for his annual barbecue picnic. It was a good opportunity for Stuart to show off Madison to those in his inner circle. The fact that Lyle and his wife, Sandy, had children around the ages of Dottie and Carrie was another good reason to accept his agent and friend's invitation.

"I'm glad you could make it," Lyle said to Stuart. He was standing over the grill in their big backyard.

"Saved me the trouble of firing up my own grill," Stuart half joked, holding a can of beer.

"Hey, you and your brood are welcome anytime. That includes your new significant other."

"I appreciate that," Stuart said, glancing over at Madison. She was giving the girls her full attention, and they were eating it up.

"So just how significant is she in your life?" Lyle asked as turned over some baby back ribs.

"Pretty damned significant."

"Significant enough that you might be thinking about marrying her?"

Stuart sipped his beer thoughtfully. He and Madison hadn't broached that subject, but he certainly wasn't averse to the idea. He would love to marry someone who adored his girls and him. From every indication, Madison fit the bill. But was that what she wanted? Or was she happy just dating without the major commitment?

"That's a possibility," he told Lyle. "Right now, we're just taking it day by day and seeing where things go."

"Nothing wrong with that," Lyle said. "No hurry. But clearly you're on to something here, buddy. Madison is certainly a gorgeous woman and your kids can't seem to get away from her, so she must be doing something right, aside from making you look great in her magazine."

Stuart chuckled. "Yeah, she's done a lot for my book."

"Well, if you ever do pop the question, Sandy and I would be happy to have your reception here."

"That would be wonderful. I really appreciate the offer," Stuart said.

"Hey, I've got a vested interest in keeping my best client happy," Lyle said, grinning.

"I'm more than happy with you as my agent," Stuart assured him.

"I feel the same way having you as my client," Lyle said. "The offer still stands."

"If it comes to that, we'll talk." He didn't want to look too far ahead at this point.

Madison finally got Dottie and Carrie to go play with the other children, though they seemed more than content to hang around her. While certainly flattered, she didn't want to take up all their time. Even though she enjoyed being with Stuart's well-behaved kids.

"They're so cute."

Madison turned and saw Sandy Creighton approaching with two tall glasses of lemonade.

"Yes, they are," Madison said, watching her look at the girls at play.

"Thought you might like something cold to drink," Sandy said, handing her a glass.

"Thank you." Madison smiled at the short, pretty red-haired woman in her early forties.

Sandy glanced toward the grill. "Looks like Lyle and Stuart are doing their usual shoptalk. Guess they just can't get away from it in their business."

"From what I understand, they have a pretty successful collaboration going," Madison said.

"They do. But there's a time for everything."

"Very true." Madison tasted the lemonade.

"I'm so happy that Stuart found someone to be with," Sandy said, brushing strands of hair from her face. "In spite of all his success, something has been missing since he's been on his own."

"I'm happy that he's come into my life," Madison said. "Stuart's such a gentleman, and he makes his kids his top priority. You don't find that in many men these days."

"I know," Sandy said. "Lyle's like that, too."

"I'm starting to feel strongly about Stuart," Madison admitted. "I understand, though, that the children come first and his career is very important to him, too, as it should be."

"Hey, there's plenty of room in his life for you as well," Sandy said. "And my guess is that he understands that and will see to it that you get the respect and appreciation deserved."

Madison blushed. "I'm sure you're right." She had seen nothing to suggest otherwise. Stuart, along with his girls, was rapidly becoming an integral part of her life, and she wouldn't trade it for anything.

"Right about what?" She heard Stuart's voice.

Madison turned and saw him over her shoulder.

"Just girl talk," Sandy said, winking at her. "See you later."

Madison smiled as she walked away and turned to Stuart. "Having fun?"

"Yes, with you here." He glanced toward Sandy who had joined her husband. "Looks like you've got a new friend."

"I believe I do," Madison said. She gazed into his eyes and, on the spur of the moment, decided to kiss him.

Stuart tasted her lips. "Mmm… What did I do to deserve that?"

She batted her lashes. "Do I need to count the reasons?"

A grin lifted his cheeks. "No, but I think I need to count the ways I'm lucky after finding you to make my life complete."

"That definitely works both ways," she said.

Stuart took the initiative this time to kiss her, not caring if anyone was watching.

That night, after the girls were asleep, Stuart and Madison made love in his bed. They both tried to keep the noise of intimacy down to a minimum while still expressing their desire for one another.

Stuart was wedged deeply inside Madison, and she quietly inhaled as her orgasm came just moments before Stuart climaxed. Their spent bodies clung to each other, trembling as the mutual gratification brought them to the mountain's peak and down to the waning moments of sexual ecstasy.

As she lay on top of him, Madison heard the soft words in her ear she had been waiting for: "I'm in love with you, darling."

She lifted up and looked at his face. "I love you, too."

"Really?" Stuart's hands rested on her buttocks as his heart skipped a beat.

"Yes, really," she told him. "You make it very easy to love you—and your incredible daughters."

"The same is equally true about loving you," he said. "I'm pretty sure Carrie and Dottie feel the same way."

Madison's pulse raced at the thought and her heart filled with joy. She put her face down to Stuart's and began to kiss him passionately, as fresh desire surged through her.

Chapter 17

On Saturday, Madison stood along the crowded parade route with Stuart and the girls watching the Grand Floral Parade, the crown jewel of Portland's annual Rose Festival. It was exciting for Madison to experience her first parade in the city, especially when she saw the joy it brought to Dottie and Carrie as they celebrated their eighth birthday. They watched as giant floats and local dignitaries passed by, groups sang a cappella and showed off their dance moves, and equestrian performers and marching bands delighted the throngs of onlookers.

"This is wonderful," Madison told Stuart while they held hands.

"It's a nice way to promote the city and the many

things we have to offer," he said proudly. "The girls are certainly transfixed by the parade every year."

"I'll bet." She gazed at them happily as they giggled and pointed at things. Looking back at their father, Madison asked, "Have you ever participated, since you're somewhat of a local celebrity?"

He smiled. "As a matter of fact, last year I was part of the parade. I actually sat in a convertible with the mayor."

"Look at you," she said, laughing. "Is the mayor a personal friend of yours?"

"Not really," he said. "We both just happened to cross paths at one point and one thing led to another. The truth is I'm much more at home watching the festivities with my girls, and my new girl."

Madison colored. "Well, your new girl wouldn't want to be anywhere else or with anyone else."

Stuart grinned and gave her a kiss. He wanted her to know just how important she had become in his life. And his kids had practically already adopted Madison as their mother, which she seemed to embrace just as heartily. In his mind, it was only a matter of time before they made this official and he asked Madison to marry him. He had seriously wondered for a long time if he would ever tie the knot again, and she had turned those thoughts upside down.

He hoped she also found him more than worthy of being her husband.

"Oh, look." Madison got his attention as a colorful float made its way past them.

Stuart grinned in awe and gave her a soft kiss on the forehead.

After picking up some ice cream and a cake for Carrie and Dottie's birthday, Stuart drove home. He was happy that Madison was here to celebrate his daughters' very special day. If he had his way, she would be by his side on many more such occasions.

They gathered around the dining room table. There were sixteen lit candles on the caramel cake, eight for each girl. After making a silent wish, Carrie blew out her candles and Dottie followed.

Stuart and Madison gave the girls a big hug and kiss, and then served the cake and ice cream.

Madison felt more at home than ever as she sat at the table with the closest thing she had to a real family of her own.

When the doorbell rang, Madison volunteered to answer it. "Keep eating," she told everyone. "I suspect some of your friends are stopping by to wish you a happy birthday."

She opened the door and saw a well-dressed, tall, attractive woman with high cheekbones and long, layered brown hair that matched her eyes. A linen handbag was strapped across one shoulder.

"May I help you?" Madison asked.

The woman batted curly lashes at her. "Is Stuart here?"

"Yes." Madison was about to ask her to wait while she went to get him, but the woman briskly sidestepped her and came inside.

Madison turned around to see that Stuart and the girls had stopped eating and laughing when they caught sight of the woman. Stuart quickly rose from his seat.

"What the hell are you doing here?" he asked.

"Mommy…?" The word rang from Dottie's mouth.

"Yes, it's me, honey," she responded, smiling. "I've come home—"

Stuart's jaw dropped as he watched Fawn hug Carrie and Dottie as if no time had passed.

He favored Madison with a bleak look, not even wanting to imagine what she was thinking about this sudden appearance from his ex-wife.

"You didn't answer my question," Stuart snapped at her.

She met his eyes unblinkingly. "Why do you think? I wanted to be here for my girls' birthday." Fawn removed two small wrapped gifts from her bag, handing one to Dottie and one to Carrie. They looked at them as though they were foreign objects. "Don't be shy," she said. "Open them."

"I don't want it," Dottie said, sticking out her arm to hand it back.

"Me either," Carrie seconded.

Fawn looked stunned. She glared at Madison and then Stuart before taking the gifts. "I'll put them on the table in case you change your mind later."

"They won't," Stuart said, "and neither will I. You can't just show up out of nowhere and expect us to greet you with open arms."

Fawn shot him a hard look. "Why not? Whether you like it or not, they are still my babies."

"They are hardly babies anymore," he said, frowning. The frown left his face when Stuart looked at his daughters. "Why don't you go up to your rooms, girls?"

"Why do we have to?" Carrie protested.

"Just do it."

"Why don't you make *her* leave?" Dottie asked him.

"I will," he assured her. "Soon. Now go. I'll be up shortly."

Reluctantly, the girls obeyed. Madison felt helpless. She wished she could reach out to the girls, but she wasn't sure it was her place under the circumstances.

Fawn took a deep breath as she looked at Stuart. "I know you must hate me, but if you just give me a chance, I'm sure we can be a family again." She locked eyes with Madison again.

Madison's heart sank upon hearing the words *family again*. She was speechless. *Where does that leave me?* she wondered. She looked at Stuart and saw that his expression had softened. Was Fawn's manipulation working on him? And how could she fight their history and the fact that Fawn was the girls' real mother?

She gazed at Stuart. "I think I should go and let you deal with this...."

His brow furrowed. "You don't have to."

"I think that's a good idea," Fawn interjected.

Madison bit her tongue to refrain from responding. Instead, she looked at Stuart for guidance.

"Maybe you should go," he told her. He hated to say it. But the more he thought about it, the more he feared that playing this out in front of Madison might be just what Fawn wanted to drive a wedge between them. As if she hadn't already with her unexpected presence.

"Fine," Madison said, feeling a little disappointed. She had hoped he would ask Fawn to leave instead.

"I'll drive you."

"I'll walk. I need the fresh air," she told him. Fortunately, she had worn her flats for the parade, so walking a few blocks would not be a problem.

Stuart could tell that this situation rubbed her the wrong way and he completely understood. But now that Fawn had decided to show up, he had to deal with her, for the sake of his children.

He walked Madison to the door. "I'm sorry," he said softly. "Believe me when I tell you the last person I expected to see today—or any other day for that matter—was her."

She met his eyes. "That doesn't really change the situation, does it?"

Madison looked at Fawn, who seemed to be gloating, and walked out the door, wondering if she would ever set foot in his house again.

Chapter 18

Stuart rounded on his ex-wife, not believing she actually had the nerve to show her face in his house after leaving them years ago. Now she had disrupted the life he had carefully crafted with the girls and Madison. And why? What could she possibly want from any of them at this point?

He wasn't about to give Fawn much time to explain herself, either. "You've got five minutes," he told her in his sternest voice. "Then I want you out of my house and out of my life!"

Fawn stepped closer to him. "You look good, Stuart," she said in a seductive voice. "Life has obviously treated you well."

He gave her the once-over and admitted, if only to

himself, that she was still gorgeous. But that was hardly enough to change the way he felt about her. In fact, he didn't feel anything for her, other than pity.

"I'm not interested in your compliments," he said stiffly.

She fluttered her lashes. "I can't believe the girls have grown up so much."

"What did you expect, that they would stay locked up in a damned time capsule and look the same way they did when you ran off?"

"I deserve that," she muttered. "Still, it's nice to see that you've taken good care of them."

He rolled his eyes. "Of course I did, no thanks to you."

Fawn sighed. "You can't say anything to me that I haven't already said to myself a thousand times."

Stuart's brow creased. "In that case, we really have nothing left to talk about...."

"Why don't we talk about *her?*"

"Who?" he asked, though he suspected her answer.

"That woman who just left," she said bluntly.

"She's none of your damned business!"

Fawn folded her arms defiantly. "She is if she's going to be a part of my daughters' lives."

Stuart might have laughed if this wasn't so ridiculous. Did she really think she could come there and dictate how he raised the children she had abandoned?

"First of all, you have absolutely no say in my personal life. And you sure as hell are in no position to tell me who my kids can and can't be around."

"Uh, excuse me, but they're my kids, too, whether you like it or not," she said.

His brows knitted. "Excuse *me,* but the court granted me full custody when you abandoned ship. You can't put the genie back in the bottle. You might as well go back to whatever hole you crawled out of and leave us alone." Admittedly, he had been a bit harsh, but he didn't want her to think for one second that all would be forgiven and forgotten. He peeked at his watch. "Your time is up...."

Fawn reached up and touched the side of his face. "I never should have walked out on you and the girls the way I did. I'm sorry for that."

He stepped away from her hand. "You're years too late for empty apologies."

"It's never too late to express regrets," she said. "I want you back."

His head snapped backward. "What...?"

"You heard me. I want us to be a family again. At least say you'll think about it, for the girls' sake."

Stuart wouldn't waste one second thinking about something so absurd. "It's for the girls' sake that I'd never put them through that again," he said. "We're over and have been for a long time. If you really want to do right by the girls, you'll do us all a favor and leave this town and never come back."

Fawn pursed her lips. "If that's the way you feel." She paused. "Or is it that bitch that's messing with your head?"

Stuart held his ground. "The only one messing with my head is you. Now get out of here."

She stepped forward, getting close to his face. "This isn't over!" she spat.

He sucked in a deep breath as she stormed out, leaving him a bit shaken. The last thing he needed was trouble from her that would hurt the girls or his involvement with Madison.

He hoped she would back off for everyone's sake.

Stuart headed upstairs, knowing he faced the difficult task of trying to explain to Dottie and Carrie again why Fawn had left them in the first place and, worse, why she had ever bothered to return. In both instances, he wasn't clear on the answer. He only knew that he had to protect them all over again and reassure them that their lives would still go forward. He hoped they would continue to be open to having Madison show them the love they deserved.

That was, assuming Madison still wanted that role now that Fawn had come back to try and take it away.

As expected after Fawn's dramatic appearance, Stuart found Dottie and Carrie huddled in bed together. He walked over to them, unsure what to say and not wanting to say the wrong thing.

"Are you asleep?" he asked softly.

Both girls looked up at Stuart.

"Is she gone?" Dottie asked.

He nodded. "Yes."

"Is she coming back?" Carrie asked.

"Probably at some point," Stuart said honestly, sitting on the bed.

Dottie frowned. "Why doesn't she leave us alone?"

"I'm asking myself the same question," Stuart said. "Guess she just wanted to see you girls."

"We don't want to see her," Carrie said.

"I'm afraid that may be unavoidable," Stuart told them. "Hopefully, we can just let her know that we're happier without her, and it will be enough for her." Or, he wondered, would she try to ruin that, too?

Dottie sat up. "What about Madison?"

Stuart scratched his nose. "What about her?"

"Things don't have to change with her now that Mommy came back, do they?"

He sighed. "If you're asking if I want to get back with your mother now that she showed up, the answer is a big NO." He smiled at the girls. "As far as I'm concerned, nothing has to change with Madison. She's a very important part of our lives."

Dottie smiled. "That's good. I really like her."

"Me, too," said Carrie.

"Then we're all on the same page," Stuart said, "because I really like her, too."

Carrie grinned. "We know. She likes you a lot, too."

He smiled. "I'm counting on that."

"Don't let Mommy ruin things," Dottie said, pouting.

"I won't," Stuart promised. Not if he had anything to do with it. "We'll talk about it some more tomorrow. Time to get some sleep."

"But we didn't finish our ice cream and cake," Carrie complained. "The ice cream's probably all melted by now."

"If so, we'll get more tomorrow," Stuart said, rising to his feet. "I'm sure you would agree that no one's really in the mood to start the party again tonight."

"Yeah, I'm not," Dottie said.

"I'm not either," her sister said.

Stuart leaned down and kissed both girls good-night.

It was only after he left the room that he thought more about how disappointed he was with Fawn. Obviously, she hadn't changed from the self-centered bitch who'd left him for another man and a new life. Ruining the girls' birthday was about as selfish as it got.

I'll be damned if I'll let her ever hurt them again, he thought. Once in a lifetime was enough.

Stuart's thoughts turned to Madison. She had left in somewhat of a huff, refusing to allow him to take her home. That had fed right into Fawn's manipulative hands. Whatever it took, he would assure Madison that she didn't have anything to worry about with Fawn.

What he had with Madison was more real than anything he had ever had with Fawn. The sooner she knew that, the better. Then they could get back to where they were and work on a future together.

That night, Madison tossed and turned in bed, unable to sleep. She envisioned Stuart sweeping Fawn off her feet, as he once must have, and rekindling their love. But if that were the case, where would it leave her? Would Stuart and Fawn wind up being one big happy family again?

Don't be silly, she told herself. *Just because Stuart's ex shows up out of the blue doesn't mean he'll fall for her again.*

But anything was possible, right? Especially if his ex threw herself at him. Something told Madison that Fawn had come back to town with a purpose in mind and that Stuart was right in the center of it.

Suddenly the fear of rejection Madison once had threatened to resurface. Could the great love of her life blow up in smoke? Or was this a nightmare that could still go away?

The doorbell ringing gave Madison a start. She glanced at the clock on her nightstand and saw that it was a quarter past eleven o'clock. Slipping into her robe, she ambled down the stairs barefoot. She looked through the peephole and saw Stuart standing there.

She removed the chain, unlocked the door and opened it. "Did you get your problem resolved?" she asked.

"Marry me," Stuart said simply.

"Excuse me…?" Madison had heard the words quite clearly. But digesting them was a different matter altogether.

"Let's get married," he said, shooting past her and watching as she closed the door and approached him.

"Why?" She widened her eyes at him.

"Why? Because I love you and want us to be together with my daughters."

"I understand that, but why now?" she asked, as if the answer wasn't obvious.

It was a good question and Stuart did not want to lie about it. "I just think it's a good time to make our feelings for each other official and legal," he said evenly.

As much as Madison wanted to believe that, the timing was just a little suspicious. "I can't marry you," she said.

Stuart lifted a brow. "What?"

"You heard me. This isn't a good idea."

He frowned. "Why the hell not? I thought we were in love."

"We are," she conceded. "But asking me to marry you after your ex shows up unexpectedly is not the way I want to get engaged."

"This has nothing to do with her," he insisted. She was wearing a short chenille robe, and he couldn't help but notice how sexy she looked.

"It has everything to do with her," Madison said. "She disrupts the birthday party for your daughters and the same night you ask me to marry you? I don't think so."

"So what? You think I asked you to marry me just to keep her away from the girls?" he asked. "I have full custody of them."

"I know that." Madison gave him a hard look. "She wants you back, doesn't she?" The words Fawn had said rang in her head: *I'm sure we can be a family again.*

"Don't be ridiculous," Stuart said.

"I'm not being ridiculous," she said, an edge to her

tone. "What part of wanting to be a family again did you not get? I got it all. Fawn came back to town for you and her children. How do you expect me to feel?"

"I expect you to trust me and my feelings for you," he told her flatly. "I don't give a damn what crazy thoughts Fawn has in her head. There's only one woman I want to be with, and I'm looking at her."

A spasm of warmth crept between Madison's thighs at that moment, but she suppressed it. She didn't want to lose perspective on this situation, no matter how much she wanted to be with him.

"I'm afraid that's not enough," she told him.

"So what are you saying?" Stuart stepped closer to her. He hadn't expected her to reject his proposal. What was he supposed to do now?

She sighed. "I'm saying that you need to get whatever it is that still exists between you and Fawn totally resolved if there's going to be a real future for us," Madison said. "And don't tell me there's nothing there, because I could see that there was to some degree. And as long as she has that hanging over you, it will hang over us as a couple. Also, it wouldn't be fair to Dottie and Carrie if we just tried to ignore your ex-wife's presence and pretend she doesn't exist. The girls have had enough confusion and disappointment in their lives. Trying to compete with their real mother for their affection would only make matters worse for them and me." She paused. "I'm sorry, Stuart, but I won't put them though that, and I won't put myself through that."

Stuart wanted to leave it at that, but couldn't. He held

Madison's shoulders and planted a strong kiss on her mouth, hoping it would show her that they were worth fighting for, no matter the obstacles.

Madison's nipples tingled from the mouth-watering kiss, leaving her breathless and wanting much more. But, given the circumstances, she fought off the strong desire to fall into Stuart's arms, make love to him and forget everything else.

Using all of her inner strength, she released her mouth from his and backed away. Her voice shook as she said, "You should leave."

"Let's talk about this—" he said.

"Let's not," Madison told him. "Just go and be there for your girls when they wake up in the morning. Or is your ex there to take care of them?"

Madison wished she hadn't said that last comment. But whatever the case, she suspected that Fawn was not going away quietly.

"She gave up that right a long time ago." Stuart's voice deepened. "I won't allow her to interfere with their lives and send them spiraling in the wrong direction again."

He looked at Madison's beautiful face, wanting more than anything to take her in his arms, make love to her and forget that Fawn had ever been there. But he knew that was not possible. He couldn't push Madison now and risk losing her altogether.

Stuart did as Madison had asked and left, uncertain of where he—or they—went from there.

Listening as his car drove off, Madison wondered

how a day that had begun with such promise could be
ending with such uncertainly. Why did Fawn have to
show up and put a damper on everything?

I've never been very good at competing for a man,
she thought. So why should this be any different?

She drank a glass of water and then went back to
bed. Had she really turned down an offer of marriage
from the best man she'd ever known? Wasn't that what
she had wanted?

Yes, but not when it seemed more like an act of des-
peration than desire, she told herself. Marriage under
those circumstances was bound to have trouble down
the line. When she tied the knot, she wanted it to be
for life.

Could Stuart say the same while the specter of his
ex hung over them like a dark cloud?

Madison fell asleep on that dreary thought, unsure
what tomorrow would bring.

Chapter 19

"You're kidding, right?" Holly asked during their video conversation on Sunday.

"I only wish I were," Stuart said. He'd called her to vent about Fawn's ill-timed appearance. "She's in Portland."

Holly made a face. "That woman's got some nerve. What on earth made her think she could just waltz in there like it was just another day?"

"Delusional, I guess," he muttered.

"I hope you told her where to go?"

"Yeah, anywhere but here." Stuart sipped his green tea. "Unfortunately, I don't think she listened."

"I'm so sorry," Holly told him. "I can only imagine what seeing her did to the girls."

"They weren't very happy about it," he confirmed.

"And why should they be after what she did to them?"

"I know," he said, taking a breath. "But it is what it is."

"So what did she want anyway? Or shouldn't I ask?"

"She wants us to get back together," Stuart replied.

"She what?" Holly rolled her eyes.

"That was the clear impression she gave before I told her not to even think about that happening in this lifetime and kicked her out of the house."

Holly smiled. "Good for you. The last thing you need is to waste your time on someone who isn't worth it on any level."

"You're preaching to the choir," Stuart said.

Holly paused. "How did Madison react to Fawn's presence?"

His brow creased. "How do you think?"

"I hope you assured her that Fawn was strictly in your past and that Madison was your present and future?"

"I tried to…."

"But she still got bent out of shape by it?" Holly surmised.

"Something like that." Stuart sighed. "I asked Madison to marry me…."

"Really?" Holly's eyes grew. "Did she say yes?"

He frowned. "No, she didn't. This situation with Fawn threw her—us—off track."

"Then find a way to get back on track," she said.

"I told her that I have no feelings left for Fawn and want us to be a family with the kids, but Madison didn't buy it," he said. "I don't know, I guess she thinks that somehow Fawn and I will end up back together, as silly as that sounds."

"It doesn't sound so silly to me," Holly said. "She's scared, Stuart. After already losing someone she was engaged to, the last thing she wants is to become engaged again with an ex-wife hanging around, eager to get you back."

"So what can I do?" he asked. "I can't force Fawn to get out of town, even if I wish to hell she would. And I can't alter Madison's history with Anderson any more than I can my own with Fawn. I asked Madison to trust me and allow our lives to move forward. She doesn't seem willing to do that. At this point, the ball's in her court—"

"This isn't a tennis match, for heaven's sake!" Holly said. "You can't just give up on someone you're obviously in love with. As to what you can do, you can keep working on Madison, for starters. Convince her that your love is real and you truly want her to become your wife and a mother to your children. Yes, I know she's not their real mother, but Fawn doesn't care about those kids. She's just using them as a tool to try and get what she wants."

"Tell me something I don't know," Stuart grumbled.

"You and Madison belong together. Don't even think about turning your back on that!"

A grin formed on his lips. He always got just the advice he needed from his sister. "I won't turn my back on us," he promised. "Still, I think I need to take a step back and fix my problems with Fawn before I can fix my relationship with Madison."

Holly nodded. "You're probably right about that. Take some time to settle things once and for all with Fawn. But don't take too long. Madison, in spite of playing hardball, does not want to lose you, but she won't wait around forever for you to step up to the plate."

"I understand," he told her. "Thanks."

She forced a smile. "You've helped me more than once with my relationship dramas. The least I could do was return the favor. Even then, I won't let up on you till you and Madison are back together and making plans for another wedding in the family."

Stuart chuckled. "Got it."

When he ended the chat, Stuart felt better about things, but he knew he still had his work cut out for him if things were ever to get back to the way they were between him and Madison.

On Monday, Madison sat at her desk reading the next book she would review. She was thankful she had something to preoccupy her mind after the unexpected scenario of Stuart's ex-wife surprising them. Now Madison wasn't sure which direction to turn. Yes, she still loved Stuart and that wouldn't change anytime soon. And she would certainly marry him in a minute were the circumstances ideal, which they certainly weren't right now.

Madison heard her cell phone buzz. She picked it up and saw that it was Stuart, yet again. She declined to pick up again, not sure what to say that wouldn't make matters worse between them. She figured that if he had something to talk about that was important, he would tell her in person. Anything else, she really wasn't in the mood for.

I can't bear to hear one more thing about Fawn and what she did or didn't want, Madison thought.

She would never have done what Fawn did to her kids and ever expect she had the right to look them in the face again.

But that was something Stuart would have to reconcile. Madison could only hope he didn't allow Fawn to worm her way back into his life.

If he did, what possible future could we expect to have? she thought.

"That must be some book you're reading there," Madison heard an amused voice say.

She looked up from her desk and saw Jacinta standing there with a big smile on her face. "It's not that good," Madison said truthfully, closing the paperback. "What are you doing here?"

"I was in the area and decided it was a good time to see where my gal pal works when she's telling it like it is to all those writers."

Madison couldn't help but grin. "Well, this is it. As for the writers, yes, I tell it like it is, for better or worse."

"Like marriage," Jacinta said with a laugh. "Sometimes you don't know what hit you till it's too late."

Madison frowned pensively. "I suppose...."

"Oops. Did I say something wrong?"

"Marriage is just a sore subject for me right now," she admitted.

Jacinta batted her lashes. "Do tell...."

Madison sighed. "It's a long story."

"So let me buy you lunch, and you can tell me all about it."

Madison looked at the pile of books on her desk. "I've got a lot of work to do."

"Don't we all," Jacinta said. "You've got to eat, too."

"You're not going to take no for an answer, are you?" Madison asked.

"It's not my style," Jacinta said with a friendly smile. "I know a great soul-food restaurant not too far from here. I'll have you back in no time, but not before I hear what's got you down in the dumps."

Madison gave in, glad to have someone to share her feelings with on a tender subject.

The Rib Shack was on Delmar Street. As would be expected at this time of day, it was packed. They had to wait a few minutes before a table became available. That gave Madison some extra time to gather her thoughts as she considered her past, present and future. The greater emphasis was on her future and whether or not it was one she would share with Stuart. Or one in which she would once again have to find her own way in life.

Madison followed Jacinta's lead and ordered barbecued chicken, turnip greens, corn bread and coffee.

"So let's have it," Jacinta prodded. "What is it about marriage that has you huffing and puffing?"

"Stuart asked me to marry him," Madison said.

"Interesting, but obviously that isn't the whole story."

"I wish." Madison took a breath. "His ex-wife showed up at his house after we got back from the parade Saturday."

Jacinta's eyes bulged. "You don't mean the same wife who ran off with another guy without looking back?"

"That would be the one."

"Oh, boy, that couldn't have gone very well."

"It didn't," Madison said. "You should have seen the girls. They weren't quite sure who to turn to. But it definitely wasn't their mother."

"Could you blame them?"

"Not at all. But she shook everyone up, and we're all still feeling the effects," Madison said.

"I'll bet." Jacinta gazed at her. "So did she come for a little visit or—"

"To reclaim the family she gave up."

Jacinta's brows furrowed. "Just like that, with no warning or consideration that Stuart may be involved with someone else?"

"Fawn certainly didn't give a damn about that," Madison said irritably. "It was almost like I wasn't even in the room while she stated her plans for reestablishing her role in their lives."

Jacinta digested that. "Clearly, Stuart left no doubt as to where his head was if he proposed to you."

"Well, that's kind of a sticking point in and of itself...." Madison paused when the food arrived.

"Explain, please," Jacinta said once the waiter had moved on.

Madison wasn't sure she could in a way that didn't make her sound like a complete idiot. But she had to try. "I told Stuart I couldn't marry him while this issue with his ex-wife was still unresolved. Basically, I don't want to be caught in the middle of his love-hate relationship with the mother of his children."

Jacinta's mouth hung open. "You think he still loves the woman after what she put him through?"

"Not exactly," Madison said. "But there had to have been something there when they were married and brought two beautiful daughters into this world. Can that type of bond really just go away?"

"Will you listen to yourself, girl?" Jacinta said while buttering a piece of corn bread. "Having a bond with someone because of children is not the same as carrying any lingering feelings for the person. Do you realize how many divorces there are in this country where kids are involved?"

Madison stuck a fork in her greens. "I think I have an idea."

"Then you must know that people move on all the time, even if the ex chooses to show up for whatever reason. The point is that you're the one Stuart loves. I know it, and you know it. So why not forget about that bitch and marry the man?"

Yes, why not? Madison asked herself. She didn't doubt that they could have a great life together. And she adored the girls. But did she really want a constant reminder of his past life and love, assuming Fawn chose to stick around in Portland?

"I just think Stuart rushed into this proposal more to stave off Fawn's obvious advances than because he believed it was the right thing to do at this time."

"So what if he did?" questioned Jacinta. "The result is still the same. He wants you as his bride. Besides, Stuart doesn't strike me as the type of man to do things on impulse, even if he wants to stick it to his ex."

"Maybe you're right," Madison said. Or maybe not and Stuart had acted impulsively when he'd asked her to marry him. Perhaps once Fawn was out of the picture again, he might feel differently.

I need to know for sure that he really wants me as his wife and not just so he can escape the specter of his first wife.

Chapter 20

On Wednesday, Stuart called Grace over to watch the girls while he went out. It pained him that Madison wasn't there, as he had begun to get used to her presence in his house. He could only hope that she would realize deep down inside what he knew—that they were perfect together and could overcome any bumps in the road.

"I'm going to head out now," he told them.

"When is Madison coming over?" Carrie asked.

Stuart mused. "I'm not sure," he said truthfully. "She's been pretty busy lately—"

"She's staying away because of Mommy, isn't she?" asked Dottie.

"Your mother has nothing to do with it," Stuart lied. "Believe it or not, Madison does have a busy life outside of spending time with us. Maybe it's best that we don't get too used to having her around."

"Is she breaking up with you?" Carrie asked with a worried look on her face.

"No, we're still seeing each other," Stuart said, even if they were in the middle of a cooling-off period. "You can't get rid of her that easily. She loves you guys."

Dottie eyed him. "Does she still love you?"

"Yes," he said. It was the one thing he was certain of. Getting the other things to fall back in place was a different story altogether. "And I love her. Anyway, right now Grace is here to keep you company."

Grace smiled. "That's right. Hope we're still friends?"

Dottie grinned. "Yeah, we're still friends."

"How about you?" Grace asked Carrie. "Still friends?"

She giggled. "Yeah."

"In that case, why don't we go in the backyard and play," Grace suggested. "And your dad can be on his way."

Stuart smiled at the twins lovingly. "Give me a hug."

They did and he gave Grace a silent look of thanks for filling in for him.

In his car, Stuart got a call from his father. He put it on speaker.

"This is a surprise," Stuart said.

"I was hoping to catch you before you got too busy today," he said.

"I always have time to speak to you, Dad." Stuart

paused. "So what's up?" He assumed there was something, and he had a pretty good idea what it was.

"Your sister told me that Fawn paid you a visit," Robert said.

"Yeah, she's here," Stuart muttered.

"That must have gone well," he said.

Stuart snickered. "Yeah, we had a ball." He still couldn't believe she'd had the audacity to show up as if it was nothing. On the other hand, if nothing else, she had shown herself to be as unpredictable as ever, which caused him even more concern. For all he knew, she would actually try something brainless like seek custody of his kids. The mere thought raised his blood pressure several notches. He would never allow Carrie and Dottie to be raised by someone who had walked out of their lives at the worst possible time.

"Are you there?" Robert asked.

Stuart refocused. "Yeah, sorry."

"I was saying that I'm not surprised Fawn returned. I said all along that it was foolhardy for her to walk away from the best thing that could ever happen to her, which was you and the girls. I knew it was only a matter of time before the fun and games would run out and she'd come crawling back."

"Well, she can crawl from here to eternity and it won't get her anywhere," Stuart said firmly. "I'd have to be crazier than her if I even thought about letting her into my life again."

"She is in your life whether you want to hear that or

not," his father stressed. "Those are still her kids, and she's not about to let you forget that."

Stuart's brow creased. "So what are you saying—that I give in to her manipulation and betrayal?"

"Not at all, son. All I'm saying is that pretending she doesn't exist won't solve anything. Let her get off her chest whatever she has to say and then be mature about telling her how much she hurt you and the girls, and that that's a bridge you're never willing to cross again."

"And what if she ignores all that and still tries to get her hooks into me?" Stuart asked.

"It will be hard for her to ignore what's staring her right in the face," he said. "You've moved on and she has to do the same, for her own sake as well as for the girls."

"Hope she listens to reason," Stuart said. "Somehow I don't think she sees things as rationally as you or I do."

"Why don't you just wait and see how it goes before jumping to conclusions."

"All right." Stuart turned onto Dexter Boulevard. "Anything you say, Dad."

"I'm only saying what any father would when looking out for his child, much like you do with your own kids," Robert said.

"I know, and I appreciate it." He liked having his father being more involved in his life.

"So how's Madison holding up through all this?" Robert asked.

Stuart thought about it. "Not as well as I would have hoped," he said candidly, assuming Holly had already told him about the failed marriage proposal. "She wasn't very happy about Fawn showing up."

"That's understandable, but unavoidable. Life can be messy sometimes. I'm sure Madison realizes that as well as anyone."

"Yeah, I suppose," Stuart said musingly. "We've both been through the wringer."

"And you're still in the game," Robert said. "Whatever hiccup Fawn caused can be overcome if both of your hearts are in it."

"You're right." He wondered if both their hearts were really in it. Or was it just his?

"Did I ever tell you that your mother turned me down the first time I asked her to marry me?" Robert asked.

Stuart's eyes widened. "No, you never mentioned that."

"Well, she did."

"Why?"

"Said I caught her off guard and she said the first thing that came to her mind." He chuckled hoarsely. "Anyway, when I asked her again a week or so later, she said yes. The rest is history."

Stuart smiled, touched to hear about the beginning of his parents' journey. "I'm glad she said yes the second time around."

"So am I, believe me," he said with a laugh. "I think it'll be the same for you. Don't give up on Madison."

"I don't intend to, Dad," Stuart said.

When he hung up, Stuart dialed Madison's number. Again, she failed to pick up, leaving him confused.

Why aren't you answering? he thought. *Don't you know it's driving me crazy being apart from you? Or has everything changed now that Fawn's back in town?*

Oddly, Stuart noted that Fawn had also left him several messages that he'd chosen not to respond to.

Stuart checked his frustrations as he met Chad at the bistro on Eighteenth Avenue and gave him the rundown on his latest woes.

Chad shook his head in disbelief. "She's really here now?"

Stuart nodded. "Unless she's left town, which I seriously doubt." He took a sip of his cocktail.

"Knowing you, you really laid into her."

"You could say that," Stuart muttered. "Not that she didn't have it coming."

"She did, trust me," Chad said. "But you didn't ask to meet with me to hear what you already know. You'd like my thoughts on where to go from here...."

Stuart nodded. "Yeah, guess I could use some input from my best friend—not that I haven't already been given plenty of advice on the situation."

"I'm sure you have. I don't suppose you've tried the direct approach and told her to get lost—again?"

"She doesn't seem to want to take no for an answer, so I've tried avoiding her, hoping she'll get the message."

"That's the wrong message you want to send there," Chad said, scratching his chin. "You need to meet with her and bring the girls, too."

Stuart's brows lowered. "You can't be serious?"

"I'm very serious," he said.

"The girls want absolutely nothing to do with her."

"I'm not sure about that," Chad told him. "They're siding with you since you're the one who's always been there for them. But she's still their biological mother."

"I get that," Stuart said. "But I fail to see what meeting with her as a family will accomplish...."

"It'll give you a chance to show her that you and the girls have been fine on your own. In fact, much more than fine without her. It will also show Fawn that Dottie and Carrie still respect her as their mother, even if she's not someone they want in their lives. It could make all the difference in the world for making it clear to her that it's too late to turn back the clock."

"I see your point," Stuart said. "I think I'll give it a try."

"That's all you can do, buddy," Chad told him.

Stuart lowered his face bleakly. "Things with Madison have hit a snag because of this."

"How much of a snag?"

"She turned down my marriage proposal and hasn't been taking my calls," Stuart said. "Apparently she wants me to get the Fawn drama worked out satisfactorily before we get things going again."

Chad cocked a brow. "Sorry to hear that."

"Me, too," Stuart said. "She knows I love her and not Fawn. But Madison's chosen to take a hard stance on this."

"Didn't you say she'd been there, done that, with an engagement that went nowhere?" Chad asked.

"Yeah, but this isn't the same—" Stuart said.

"Maybe not from your point of view," Chad said. "But from hers, it's pretty similar. She's simply trying to protect herself from being hurt again."

"And what if I can't get rid of Fawn?" questioned Stuart. "Does that mean I end up being lonely and miserable again?"

Chad favored him with a straight look. "I don't see that happening. Fawn will get the message sooner or later that she's not wanted around here," he said. "As for the lonely and miserable bit, you and Madison will find your way though this one way or another. You've got that type of magic going between you that will last, no matter the potholes you're bound to encounter from time to time."

Stuart sipped his drink, feeling more confident that a little patience and a lot of faith could go a long way with Madison.

Madison rode her bike, enjoying the warm weather. With a river that ran through the city and the Cascade Mountains in the backdrop, bike riding in Portland seemed more like a laid-back adventure than an arduous task. She wished Stuart was riding with her. And perhaps the girls. But everyone needed to take a break from things till they had time to work themselves out.

The girls don't need to compete for the affection of their mother and their father's girlfriend, Madison thought. *And I have my own problems.* She didn't want to lose ground in her relationship with Stuart. Even if an engagement should be held off for now, the thought of not being with him was killing her.

When Madison got home, she did what she probably should have done a few days ago and phoned Stuart. She was dying to hear his deep and usually mellow voice. Whatever issues they had, bottling them up inside her wasn't doing either of them any good. *I owe it to him, his girls and the love I feel for them to not let Fawn upend what we have going for us,* she thought.

Stuart picked up on the first ring. "Hey," he said smoothly.

"Hi," she said softly.

"I've left you messag—"

"I got them," she acknowledged. "I've been pretty busy." She doubted he would buy that, but didn't want to make it too obvious that she had been avoiding him.

"I need to see you," he said in a low voice.

Madison sighed. "I need to see you, too."

"Can I come over?" Stuart asked huskily.

"Please do."

"See you shortly."

"I'll be waiting...."

Chapter 21

The moment Stuart stepped in the door, whatever tension had existed between him and Madison seemed to fall by the wayside.

"I..." he began.

She put a finger to his lips. "Not now—"

Madison wasted little time pulling him close and planting a lingering kiss on his mouth. Her body tingled all over, and she could only think about making love to him.

Without uttering a word, she took his hand and led him upstairs to her bedroom, where she stripped naked and then watched greedily as he did the same.

He grabbed a condom packet from his pants and opened it. But before he could put it on, she said, "No, let me..."

Stuart swallowed and closed his eyes momentarily as Madison covered his erection. Then she met his eyes to tell him she was ready to be taken to bed. He could never remember desiring her more than he did at this very moment.

Scooping Madison into his arms, Stuart carried her to the bed, laying her on the comforter where she beckoned him to get on top of her. He happily obliged, barely able to contain himself as he moved between her legs and drove into her with passion. She locked in on his manhood, squeezing him deep inside her, as if to make him her sex prisoner.

More than willing to do his share, Stuart propelled himself into her again and again, stimulated by the depths of his entry and the moans of intimacy escaping her lips. Fighting back his overpowering need for release, he brought down his mouth hard upon hers, kissing her deeply, enjoying the taste of her soft, succulent lips.

His chest rubbed against her hard nipples, causing Madison to quiver. He felt her legs wrap around his back as she brought herself to him in rapid motion.

Madison couldn't stand it anymore; she let go and felt her climax erupt in full force. Gasping deeply, she cried out as Stuart continued to thrust while she moved with the same fervor and need for appeasement.

He shook violently as she shuddered, and they both reached the height of fulfillment at once. They kissed, touched, caressed, sighed and perspired together as the moment of impact carried them into a completion that went from Madison's head right down to her toes. She clung to Stuart, needing him in every way.

When their lovemaking had died down, along with the pounding of her heart, only then did Madison speak. "I'm glad you came," she said soothingly.

"So am I." Stuart looked down at her, admiring everything he saw. "So I guess we're good then?"

She smiled. "Well, that depends…"

"On?" he asked, but guessed what was on her mind.

"Where do things stand with Fawn?" Madison almost hated to spoil the moment. But she had to know that Fawn wasn't going to come between them.

Stuart wished to hell his ex hadn't decided to show up uninvited, leaving him to clean up the mess she'd made.

"I'm taking the girls to see her tomorrow," he responded solemnly.

Madison looked at him. "You really think that's a good idea?"

He shrugged. "It seems like the best way to present a united front. At the same time, it will let Fawn know that Dottie and Carrie don't hate her, even if they don't like her very much. Maybe that will be enough to get her to turn around and go back to where she came from."

"What about her feelings for you?" Madison asked pointedly. She knew that the girls were only part of what Fawn was after.

"I think I made it perfectly clear to her after you left that night that I am very much spoken for and don't have the slightest desire to turn back the clock. If she's got any dignity left, she'll respect that."

Madison rubbed her toes on his. "And if she doesn't?"

"Then she'll be forever miserable," he said. "There is only one woman I want to spend the rest of my life with, and I'm looking at her."

"Is that so?"

"Yes, it is." Stuart kissed her shoulder, finding that he could never get enough of her. He slipped his hand between her legs. "Any complaints?"

She felt that was a question she could hardly answer with a clear head, given that they were naked and his touch was maddeningly effective.

"None whatsoever." Madison licked her lips.

Stuart decided to take full advantage of the moment and leave everything else to be considered another day. Right now, his sole focus was on the woman who not only owned his heart, but gave him every reason to believe they could get through anything.

The next day, Stuart phoned Fawn. He realized he couldn't put it off forever, and that the only way to get her off his back was to try to reason with her.

"Why did you take so damn long to return my calls?" Fawn spat angrily.

"Why do you think?" Stuart said, trying to keep his cool. "I didn't feel like playing any more games with you."

"This isn't a game, Stuart. All I want is a second

chance with you and the girls. Is that so hard to believe?"

"Yes, it is," he said. "And you can't seriously expect us to just roll over and become a family again because it's what you want."

"I know it will take some time, but—"

"But nothing," Stuart broke in. "I'm happily involved with someone else and have no plans to change that."

"What's she got that I don't?"

He nearly laughed at the question, outrageous as it was coming from her. "She's got my back, for one thing. You sure as hell never did."

"I did at one point, but you've conveniently chosen to forget," Fawn snapped.

"Can you blame me?" he shot back. "I don't want to remember anything about you that I don't have to."

"You're not being fair," she whined. "I can still give you everything you need and more."

Stuart wondered if she was really that confident or if she was simply grasping at straws.

"I don't want or need anything from you," he said. "I'm not going to break up with the lady in my life— and certainly not for my ex-wife who ditched me for another man."

"It was a mistake," Fawn said.

"Tell me something I don't know." Stuart sighed. "In any event, it's a mistake you'll have to live with. Don't make the girls pay for your sins any more than they already have."

"That's not my intention," she insisted. "There is

something called forgiveness. People make mistakes, and Carrie and Dottie will understand that over time. And so will you, if you just give us half a chance."

Stuart grimaced. This was going to be harder than he thought. Everything he said was going in one ear and out the other. But he couldn't let her rattle him, especially if he was going to face her and persuade her to leave them alone for good.

"What part of *it's over* don't you get?" Stuart asked flatly.

"So why the hell did you call me then?" Fawn asked. "To hurl insults?"

He sucked in a deep breath, realizing this was getting him nowhere and was only making matters worse. *I have to stick to the plan,* he thought, *and keep in check my annoyance.*

"Actually, I want to meet with you in person to see if we can clear the air," he said nicely. "I'd like to bring the girls, too."

"Really?" Her voice perked up.

"Yeah. It would do them some good to see you again." Or so he hoped.

"That works for me."

"I think it's best if we meet in neutral territory. There's a café not far from your hotel—let's meet there," he said.

"Fine," she said. "What time?"

"Three o'clock."

"I'll be there."

"Good. We'll see you then."

He hung up, wondering if this was the right way to go about getting her to back off. Or would he only be encouraging her to pursue this fantasy of becoming a family again?

I'll have to sell this to the girls, he thought. They had been hardened to Fawn ever since she had come back, and they felt that she had rejected them. Though Stuart understood their anger, he did not want them to carry this forever. For that matter, he didn't want to carry it forever, either.

If everything worked out right, they could have some sort of closure and get on with their lives without Fawn. But he knew all too well that things were never that easy when it came to his ex-wife.

For the sake of his kids and his love for Madison, Stuart was banking on the fact that Fawn would do right by all of them.

"I definitely wasn't expecting that," Madison said on the phone to her sister. She was sitting on the back porch, and she had just told Bianca the full tale— everything from Fawn's sudden appearance to Stuart's hasty proposal, to her rejection, to their unexpected passion last night.

"You *should* have been expecting that," Bianca said. "I'm sure you were both horny as hell, so jumping each other's bones was just unavoidable."

Madison blushed. "Probably," she conceded. She remembered how hot and heavy it had been, as if it had been a year since they had last made love. He had given her multiple orgasms and made her wonder how on earth she could survive if they were ever apart for a longer stretch. "But I actually meant that I hadn't expected Fawn to turn up like that, practically demanding that Stuart take her back."

"Bless his heart that he didn't fall into that trap," Bianca said. "I don't know what his ex was thinking if she thought that he would toss you to the curb and hook up with her again. Maybe she was on drugs or something."

"I never got that impression," Madison said. "Actually, I think she knew exactly what she was doing."

"Which makes it all the more pathetic," Bianca said. "Once you give up a man, especially one as hot and successful as Stuart, there's no turning back. Fawn made her bed and will always have to lie in it—but without Stuart. Sorry for the pun." Bianca laughed.

"Amen to that," Madison said. "But that doesn't mean she won't keep trying to dig her claws into him. How do I handle that?"

"The same way you've handled previous relationship crises—by keeping a cool head and not letting it get to you. Let her do what she can and see where it gets her. Stuart's a big boy, and he's made his choice. There is no going back for either of you."

"What about his girls?" Madison asked. "Fawn's definitely not above using them as pawns to score points with Stuart."

"The way that man feels about you, there aren't enough points out there for her to score to take away a game you've already won," Bianca said confidently.

"Just because you aren't their real mom doesn't mean they aren't sold on you. They clearly want you to be the woman who fills the shoes of a mommy figure, so go with it and don't worry about her."

"You're right, I'll try not to." As always, Madison could count on helpful advice from her sister. Now all she had to do was live it. She could not allow Fawn to mess with her head.

"As far as passing on Stuart's proposal, I might have done the same thing under the circumstances," Bianca said.

"But what if he never asks again?" Madison said. Her mind inevitably flashed back to her previous engagement that had ended up disintegrating right before her eyes. "I don't want to end up regretting—"

"Trust me. Stuart's no fool," Bianca told her. "I think he showed you last night just how much he's into you. He will definitely pop the question again at a time that will be more appropriate. Meanwhile, just keep enjoying his company and showing him how you feel about him in every way you can."

Madison grinned. "I'll do that."

"Good. And when you two get hitched, maybe you can have the honeymoon here in Las Vegas. I'd love to play host to you newlyweds."

"That might work," Madison said. But she didn't want to get too carried away. Stuart hadn't asked her to marry him again.

Chapter 22

"Why do we have to see her?" Dottie complained as Stuart told the girls his plans.

"Because she is still your mother and it's the right thing to do," he said, standing in front of them in his study.

"What are we supposed to say to her?" Carrie asked.

"Just say what you feel," Stuart responded. "But try to be nice about it."

"What if she wants us to live with her?" Dottie asked.

"That's never going to happen," he assured her. "I already made it perfectly clear that she can't have you—or me, for that matter. But she still needs to know that you girls are happy with your lives and that you're ready to forgive, if not forget the things she's done. Do you think you can do that for me?"

"I guess," she said.

"Yeah," Carrie agreed.

"That's my girls." Stuart smiled. "So let's get this over with and then we can go for ice cream afterward."

Carrie and Dottie beamed with approval.

Ten minutes later, Stuart pulled into the parking lot of the café. He thought about reminding the girls to be on their best behavior, but saw no reason to. Both were pretty smart for their age, and he knew that Fawn would see that he'd done a good job bringing them up without her help. He wanted Dottie and Carrie to see past the person who had deserted them, and see that Fawn was a mother who had made mistakes, but that she was ready to atone for at least some of them.

They walked into the café together and sat at the table where Fawn was waiting.

"Thanks for coming," Stuart said.

"Thank you for bringing the girls," she said, offering them a bright smile. "You both look so pretty."

"You do, too," Dottie told her.

"She's right," Carrie said. "Guess we look like you."

"You really do," Fawn murmured. She seemed genuinely moved by the words.

Stuart grinned guardedly and thought, *So far, so good.*

A few hours later, Stuart sat on a park bench next to Madison. He laid out the good, the bad and the ugly about the meeting with his former wife.

"She won't be pursuing child custody," he said thankfully.

Madison sneered. "She deserves a pat on the back for that."

"Yeah, I know," Stuart agreed. "She also seems to have reconciled herself with the fact that there can never be another 'us,' though I think she's keeping a glimmer of hope that the possibility still exists."

"Only in her dreams," Madison said.

"Last, but not least, it appears that Fawn is here to stay." He frowned. "Meaning she's liable to show up at any time for one reason or another, but mainly to be a pain in the ass to me as well as you—"

Madison wrinkled her nose. She had no desire to put up with an ex looking for trouble. But what could she do about it?

"Where is she?" Madison asked.

Stuart's brows lifted. "What?"

"Where is she staying?"

He told her the name of the hotel.

"I'll take care of this myself," she told him.

"Uh, what did you have in mind?"

"I'm not going to beat her up or anything," Madison promised. "I just think it's time we had a girl-to-girl talk. Don't worry about it."

"Fine," he said. "I trust that you know what you're doing."

Madison got up and Stuart moved to follow her. "Don't—" she told him. "I've got this. Sit for a while and keep enjoying this beautiful day. I'll see you later...."

He watched her walk away, contemplating his past and future colliding like two freight trains.

When Madison was out of sight, Stuart got up and walked home to be with his kids.

Madison honestly did not know exactly what she would say to Stuart's ex when they were face-to-face. She only knew that it was something she had to do, if only for peace of mind. In fact, it was more than that. She needed to set this woman straight once and for all, so she and Stuart could go about their lives without further interference.

Arriving at the hotel, she took the elevator up to Fawn's room, hoping she was there. If not, she would simply come back. She was not willing to live a life where each and every day she would be wondering if Fawn was right around the corner, waiting to drop in on them and cause trouble.

She knocked hard on the door a couple times. There was some movement inside.

The door opened and Fawn glared at her, one hand planted firmly on a hip. "What are you doing here?"

Madison took a breath, but remained strong in her resolve. "What does it look like? I came to talk to you."

Fawn wrinkled her nose. "I don't have anything to say to you."

"Then just listen, and I'll do all the talking," Madison said. Before she could lose her nerve, she made her way past Fawn and walked into the room.

Fawn shut the door and turned on Madison. "Say what you have to and get out."

Madison sighed, studying the woman who was once

Mrs. Stuart Kendall. She could see why Stuart had fallen for her. Fawn was striking, apart from her obvious personality flaws.

I better use my one opportunity to get it right, Madison thought. Otherwise, there was no telling how far Fawn might go to try and ruin Stuart's life, and hers with it.

"So now that Stuart made it perfectly clear what direction he wants to go in, what's keeping you in town?" Madison asked.

Fawn's eyes batted. "Like that's any of your business."

Madison held her hard gaze. "You made it my business when you showed up out of nowhere, trying to steal my man right in front of me."

"First of all, I didn't show up out of nowhere," Fawn said. "I just came home. Also, I didn't try to steal your man. Stuart and I were married once, and I'm the mother of his children."

"So what!" Madison snapped. "You're divorced now. And the fact that Stuart chose to marry you once doesn't give you any extended privileges as his ex-wife. And as far as his kids go, giving birth to them does not make you a mother. You need to actually be there for them through thick and thin to qualify for that title."

"I never stopped loving my daughters," Fawn said, running a hand through her hair.

"You have a funny way of showing it. Abandoning them and running off with another man is not love in my book."

Fawn pursed her lips. "What the hell would you know about it?"

"More than you think," Madison responded. "I've never had children, but I've been around enough to know that leaving them as you did can scar them for life. As far as abandonment goes, I once thought I had found the perfect man. Only he thought otherwise, and he called off our engagement and threw away everything we had."

"Sad story, but it has nothing to do with me," Fawn insisted.

"Doesn't it?" Madison argued. "You did the exact same thing to Stuart. Only it was one hundred times worse, because you were married to him. At least my heart was broken before I walked down the aisle."

Fawn lowered her gaze. "I never meant to hurt him."

"But you did," Madison said. "How did you expect him to feel then? How do you expect him to feel now?"

"I didn't really take much time to think about that," she said, sighing. "At the time, I felt trapped in my marriage, trapped being the mother of two young girls that were a handful. There were times when I thought I might go off the deep end. Then Jimmy came along. He was dark, dashing and as sexy a man as I'd ever seen. He gave me the type of attention Stuart used to give me, before his writing took over and I became second fiddle. That moved to third fiddle when the twins were born. Jimmy gave me the opportunity to be wild and crazy again like I was when Stuart and I first started dating. I loved feeling that way and being free of all the

responsibilities that go with being a wife and mother."
She paused. "When Jimmy asked me to go away with
him to travel around the world, have lots of sex and just
be myself, I took it."

Madison gazed at her, not quite expecting the story
that had come out of her mouth. "So what happened
to Jimmy?"

"He moved on to someone else who was younger,
sassier, uncomplicated," Fawn said softly. "At first, he
was everything I could have hoped for, maybe more.
But gradually that all began to change when he became
bossy, drank too much, spent money we didn't have
and developed a wandering eye that looked in every
direction except my way. After a while, I knew it was
over. He never even tried to stop me from leaving. He
seemed happy that I was doing what he'd wanted to do,
but he'd lacked the guts to come out and say it was time
for me to leave."

"So you came back here for what?" Madison asked.
"Did you think you could just pick up the pieces with
Stuart and the girls after no contact with them for
years?"

Fawn frowned and shrugged. "I really didn't have
anywhere else to go."

"You have lots of places to go," Madison told her.
"There's a whole world out there. I assume you've seen
a lot of it in your travels. You're a beautiful woman and
there are a lot of good single men out there for you to
meet. Unfortunately, Stuart is spoken for. I love him
and he loves me. Can't you respect that?"

"Yes, I can." Fawn took a breath. "But the girls will always be my daughters, no matter what poor choices I've made."

"You're right, they will always be your daughters," Madison said. "But that doesn't mean you have to stay where you're not wanted, trying to force a relationship on them that they don't want. They get it. I get it. You can certainly keep in touch with them wherever you go. In time, they might even learn to appreciate it. But, for now, your presence in their lives is not only a distraction, but it's harmful to them."

Fawn studied her thoughtfully. "And I suppose you'll be there to help them cope and make the most of their lives?"

Madison looked her in the eye. "That's certainly my intention. I would never try to step into your shoes as their birth mother, but if given a chance, I would certainly do everything in my power to show them the love and devotion they deserve. The same is true for their father, who loves them to death and has done nothing but prove that to them every single day. That is part of why I fell in love with Stuart and want to become part of his family."

"Looks like you've got it all together," Fawn said with a catch to her voice.

"I'm far from perfect," Madison told her. "Who is? But I do know what it takes to be a family. I'd like the opportunity to be a part of that household. I promise you that letting go of them would be good for everyone, including yourself. And you should look to find someone else who will give you what it takes to make you happy."

Fawn licked her lips. "All right. Go ahead and make this happy home with Stuart and the girls," she said flatly. "I won't stand in the way."

Madison smiled softly, sensing that she meant it. "Thank you."

"Just do me a favor," Fawn said.

"What?"

"Tell Dottie and Carrie that I'll always love them and will try to find a way to make up for all the pain I've caused them."

"I'll tell them. I promise."

Fawn nodded. "Then I guess you'd better go. I need to pack."

Madison considered giving her a hug for good luck but felt that might be overdoing it. But she sincerely believed that this was the best possible thing Fawn could do for herself and the family she had left behind.

"Good luck," she told Fawn.

"Same to you," Fawn said with a slight smile.

Madison counted her blessings as she left the room. She had gotten far more than she had expected from Fawn, and she was overjoyed. She took out her cell phone, eager to share the news right away with Stuart. Then she decided it would be much better to do it face-to-face.

Chapter 23

Stuart was more than a little curious as to how things were going between Madison and Fawn. He hated to think that they might have come to blows, but he was pretty sure Madison could be counted on to show restraint and act reasonably. He loved Madison for taking the initiative to deal with his ex-wife.

Stuart picked up one of his books in the study. Suddenly, he heard some commotion and turned as the girls came running into the study with their faces lit with excitement.

"What's going on?" he asked.

"Madison just drove up," Dottie yelped.

"Really?" Stuart grinned.

"I'll let her in," Carrie said.

"I'll go with you," Dottie said.

"Why don't we all go together?" Stuart said. He picked up his pace to keep up with them and hoped that Madison would have good news.

He watched as Carrie opened the door and immediately hugged Madison's waist.

"Nice to see you, too," Madison said, bending over and giving her a kiss. "You too, Dottie," she said and gave her a hug.

"Any hugs left for me?" Stuart asked, smiling.

"I think I can muster up one," Madison said, smiling back. She gave him a warm hug, and then felt his mouth on hers. The kiss lasted a few long seconds. "That was even nicer."

"For me, too," he said.

"Do you want to see our rooms?" Carrie asked. "We changed them around."

"You can tell us if we need to change even more," Dottie said.

Madison laughed. "I'd love to see your rooms. But first, I'd like to talk to your dad for a few minutes. Is that all right?"

The girls looked at each other as though trying to decide which way the conversation would go.

"I'll be up soon, I promise," she told them.

"Why don't you go up and wait for us?" Stuart said.

He watched them race toward the stairs.

"Why don't we go to my study," Stuart said, taking Madison's elbow.

"All right." She allowed him to lead her, feeling wonderful about being back in his presence and having the girls show such love to her. They were the cutest things, and she couldn't imagine not being a part of their lives.

Stuart closed the doors to the study, not wanting the girls to listen in.

"Can I get you something to drink?" Stuart asked.

"No, I'm fine, thanks," she told him.

"Okay." He thought about getting one for himself, but decided against it. "So how did it go?"

Madison lifted her chin and met his eyes. "Better than expected."

"Meaning…?" he asked.

"Meaning she's leaving," Madison told him.

"Leaving the city?"

She smiled. "Yep. And the state, too."

Stuart took a moment, wondering exactly what had gone on at the meeting. "What did you say to her?"

"Something she needed to hear," Madison said.

"Hmm… And no punches were thrown?"

"Not a single one."

He chuckled. "Just checking."

"Well, check no more," Madison told him. "Fawn's backing off and we won't have to keep wondering what her next move is."

"You want to tell me how you managed to twist her arm without touching her?" Stuart asked.

"Let's just say I appealed to her sense of reason. And it worked!"

"I'm glad to hear that." Stuart put his hand on her

shoulder. "I know the girls will be, too, though they also left her on good terms, all things considered."

Madison smiled. "That's the way it should be."

"I couldn't agree more." He tilted his face and brought their mouths together. "Thanks for standing up to Fawn."

Madison tasted his kiss, which left her tingling. "It wasn't as difficult as you might think. Like most of us, she made some wrong choices and lost her way in the process. I just helped get her on the right path. Or at least pointed her in the right direction."

"Well, thanks anyway," he said. "I love you all the more for being who you are."

"I love you for being yourself, too," she said.

He slipped his arm around her waist, drawing her closer. "I don't know what I'd ever do without you."

He released her and walked to a hidden corner of the room, then pulled out a bouquet of red roses he'd tucked away there. He handed them to her, then looked her in the eyes. "Madison Wagner, you're the best thing that ever happened to me. I got you these roses because I knew that, no matter what happened with Fawn, I wanted you to know how much I adore you."

A wave of heat swept over Madison, and she felt her eyes welling up with tears.

"And as a matter of fact," Stuart said, "I have a little something else for you, too."

"Oh…" She met his eyes with anticipation. "And what might that be?"

"Just this…" He reached into the pocket of his slacks

and removed a 14k gold ring with a 2.5 carat round-cut diamond surrounded by white diamond accents. Stuart took her hand and slipped the ring on her finger. "Madison Wagner, please do me and my girls the honor of becoming my wife."

"Why, yes, Mr. Stuart Kendall, I would love to become your wife, and I promise to always be there for Carrie and Dottie."

Madison beamed. The ring couldn't have been more perfect. "It's beautiful," she gushed.

"You're beautiful," he said.

"How long have you been carrying this around?"

"Since the last time I asked you to marry me," Stuart said slyly. "I wanted to be ready whenever you were ready to say yes."

"And what if I never had? Would you have given it to someone else?"

He chuckled. "If you're asking if I would've gone back to my ex-wife, not a chance. There could never be another woman I want more as my wife than you."

Her heart skipped a beat. "You really mean that, don't you?"

"With every fiber in me," he said. "I love you, Madison, and not marrying you was never an option."

"Pretty confident, aren't you?" she teased him.

"I'd prefer to call it believing in us," he said. "And no matter how long that took, I was prepared to wait it out."

"Well, you won't have to wait it out anymore." Madison gazed at the sparkle in her ring, then looked up at his face. "I can't wait to become your wife."

"So let's not wait. Why don't we make it happen as soon as possible?"

"Meaning?" She met his eyes.

"We can get married at city hall next week and start to live our lives as newlyweds."

"But what about family, friends, planning, my wedding dress, etcetera?" Madison asked. "Would we live here, buy a place of our own...?"

"We can have a big reception later and invite the whole world, if you want," Stuart told her. "All we need to tie the knot is each other, the girls and maybe Chad and Jacinta, if you'd like, as witnesses. As for a wedding dress, you would look stunning in any dress. But if you insist on one, I'm sure there's enough time to get something that you love. And it doesn't matter to me if we live here, somewhere new—hell, we can even move to your town house if you want. I just want to be with you."

Madison chuckled at the idea of moving from this grand old Victorian to her much smaller town house. She gave him a steady look. "Hmm... You're really serious, aren't you?"

He nodded. "I've never been more serious about anything in my life. Making you my lawfully wedded wife means more to me than I could say. I'm sure the girls would be just as enthusiastic to have you as their mom."

The idea was starting to grow on Madison. She loved Stuart so much and the kids, too, so why should they wait to make their family official?

"Well, if Dottie and Carrie are truly on board with it, then I say let's do it," Madison declared.

"Yeah, let's," Stuart agreed. He was confident they would have the full support of his daughters. He wrapped his arms around Madison, then tilted her and laid a big kiss on her lips. "I love you."

"Wow, with a kiss like that, you must!" she joked. "I love you, too. Now let's go see what Carrie and Dottie have to say about all this."

Stuart took her hand. They headed upstairs and found the girls in Dottie's room, waiting in anticipation.

"What do you think of the room?" Dottie asked Madison anxiously.

Madison looked around at the rearranged furnishings. "I think it's great," she said. She could imagine living there herself, in their perfect house with their perfect children.

Dottie looked up at her. "Really?"

"Yes, really." Madison smiled at her. "I love the way you changed it."

Dottie blushed and glanced at Stuart, who was pleased that Madison's opinion had become so important to them. She would definitely do wonders in their family.

Carrie took her hand. "Come and see my room."

Madison was led to her room and saw similar changes. "It's wonderful," she told her. "It's good to know you both put so much work into turning your rooms into little palaces."

"Thanks," Carrie said with a bright smile.

"And you probably had a little help from your dad."

"Actually, they did it all by themselves," Stuart said

proudly. "But they might need a woman's touch the next time around."

"We would," Dottie told her emphatically.

Madison smiled. "I'll be happy to help out whenever you need me."

"Does that mean you're going to be around a lot?" Carrie asked hopefully.

Madison turned to Stuart. "Well, that's the plan...." She left it up to him to take it from there.

With that cue, Stuart grabbed her hand and showed them the ring. "We have some news for you...."

The girls gathered around them before Dottie said, "We know you asked Madison to marry you."

He cocked a brow and grinned. "How did you know?"

"We figured you would get around to it sooner or later." She giggled. "Sooner was better."

Carrie touched the ring on Madison's finger. "You must have said yes."

"I did." A smile played on Madison's lips. "But before we make it official, we wanted to make sure that this was something you guys wanted as much as we do."

The girls looked at each other, then they both took Madison's hands. "Of course it is," Carrie said.

"We'd really love for you to be our new mom," Dottie added enthusiastically.

Madison choked up and tried to keep from bawling. "And I'd love nothing more than to be your new mom and your dad's new wife."

Stuart joined them in a group hug. "Then it's settled. We're about to become a family." Stuart couldn't be happier. He gave Madison a kiss to punctuate their official engagement.

Madison couldn't help but cry for the moment. Stuart and the girls had come to mean so much to her, and she was ready to make their happy family official.

Two weeks after getting married, Madison and Stuart enjoyed their honeymoon in Las Vegas, staying in an elegant suite at the Paris Las Vegas Hotel. Bianca had suggested that the place was an ideal romantic getaway for two lovebirds. The newlyweds marveled at the hotel's 541-foot replica of the Eiffel Tower as they took the glass elevator to the top.

"I've always wanted to go to Paris," Madison told Stuart. "I'd say this is a step in the right direction."

On the observation deck, Stuart wrapped his arm around Madison's waist and held her close as they took in the amazing lights of the city at night.

"It's wonderful," cooed Madison. "Especially when I'm experiencing it with my handsome husband."

"It's just as wonderful as you are," he said. He turned her around and planted a kiss solidly on her mouth.

Madison was breathless as she kissed him back fervently, caught up in the glamour of the surroundings and the love she felt for this man. She had never been happier, and she was sure it showed.

Back in their room, they stripped off their clothes and made passionate love as though it were the first time. Stuart wedged himself deep inside Madison as she lay beneath him, her legs wrapped firmly around his back. She urged him on with each stroke.

Madison's nipples ached with raw pleasure as Stuart's hard chest stimulated them torturously. She peppered his mouth with kisses, slipping her tongue inside to taste him.

Before long, Madison had moved on top while Stuart remained deep inside her, his fullness exciting her. Their hearts raced like never before. She held his broad shoulders and moved up and down him fluidly, basking in the scent of their sex and the ecstasy of their love.

When the time came to climax, they did so together, as their breathing quickened and their bodies shook. The moment had all the power of ultimate fulfillment that came with being husband and wife for a lifetime.

* * * * *

New York Times **bestselling author**

BRENDA JACKSON

invites you to enjoy the Westmoreland family with this fabulous 2-in-1 novel...

FLAMES OF ATTRACTION

In *Quade's Babies,* Quade Westmoreland is driven by sensual memories and one incriminating photo of his one-night stand. Almost a year later, the sexy operative finally tracks her down—and discovers three little babies who look just like him!

In *Tall, Dark...Westmoreland,* Olivia Jeffries gets her longing for a taste of the wild and reckless when she meets a handsome stranger at a masquerade ball. But things get complicated when she discovers that her new lover is Reginald Westmoreland—her father's most-hated rival.

"Sexy and sizzling."
—*Library Journal* on *Intimate Seduction*

HARLEQUIN®
™ www.Harlequin.com

Pick up your copy on
Mach 26, 2013!

KPBJI300413

Escape
WITH
ME

JANICE SIMS

To escape the media firestorm surrounding her late husband, designer Lana Corday flees to an idyllic seaside. It's the perfect place for a fresh start…especially when she meets sexy hunk Tennison West. But getting Lana to let down her guard will take patience…and passion. Is he a man she can rely on…or just another disappointment waiting to happen?

"Compelling characters with unusual occupations, a terrific setting and great secondary characters showcase Sims' talent for penning great stories." —RT Book Reviews *on* Temptation's Song

⬥ HARLEQUIN®
™ www.Harlequin.com

Available April 2013
wherever books are sold!

KPJS3020413

Undeniable passion that is forbidden…

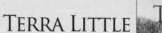
TERRA LITTLE

Gossip columnist Vanessa Valentino is forced to return back home after digging up one scandalous secret too many. Now she must face Nathaniel Woodberry—her sworn enemy! Yet Vanessa can't turn off her longing for the irresistible investigative journalist. And he can't help but seduce the former Southern belle with a healthy dose of down-home passion.

REQUEST YOUR FREE BOOKS!

2 FREE NOVELS PLUS 2 *FREE GIFTS!*

KIMANI
ROMANCE
™

Love's ultimate destination!

YES! Please send me 2 FREE Kimani™ Romance novels and my 2 FREE gifts (gifts are worth about $10). After receiving them, if I don't wish to receive any more books, I can return the shipping statement marked "cancel." If I don't cancel, I will receive 4 brand-new novels every month and be billed just $4.94 per book in the U.S. or $5.49 per book in Canada. That's a savings of at least 21% off the cover price. It's quite a bargain! Shipping and handling is just 50¢ per book in the U.S. and 75¢ per book in Canada.* I understand that accepting the 2 free books and gifts places me under no obligation to buy anything. I can always return a shipment and cancel at any time. Even if I never buy another book, the two free books and gifts are mine to keep forever.

168/368 XDN FVUK

Name   (PLEASE PRINT)

Address   Apt. #

City   State/Prov.   Zip/Postal Code

Signature (if under 18, a parent or guardian must sign)

Mail to the **Harlequin®** Reader Service:
IN U.S.A.: P.O. Box 1867, Buffalo, NY 14240-1867
IN CANADA: P.O. Box 609, Fort Erie, Ontario L2A 5X3

Want to try two free books from another line?
Call 1-800-873-8635 or visit www.ReaderService.com.

* Terms and prices subject to change without notice. Prices do not include applicable taxes. Sales tax applicable in N.Y. Canadian residents will be charged applicable taxes. Offer not valid in Quebec. This offer is limited to one order per household. Not valid for current subscribers to Kimani Romance books. All orders subject to credit approval. Credit or debit balances in a customer's account(s) may be offset by any other outstanding balance owed by or to the customer. Please allow 4 to 6 weeks for delivery. Offer available while quantities last.

Your Privacy—The Harlequin® Reader Service is committed to protecting your privacy. Our Privacy Policy is available online at www.ReaderService.com or upon request from the Harlequin Reader Service.

We make a portion of our mailing list available to reputable third parties that offer products we believe may interest you. If you prefer that we not exchange your name with third parties, or if you wish to clarify or modify your communication preferences, please visit us at www.ReaderService.com/consumerchoice or write to us at Harlequin Reader Service Preference Service, P.O. Box 9062, Buffalo, NY 14269. Include your complete name and address.

KROM13

The second book in the Hideaway Wedding trilogy…

Award-winning author

ROCHELLE ALERS

NATIONAL BESTSELLING AUTHOR

ROCHELLE ALERS

Eternal VOWS

A HIDEAWAY WEDDING

Eternal VOWS

Twins Ana and Jason and their cousin Nicholas are successful thirtysomethings who are single—and loving it. They have no idea that their relatives are betting on which one of them will get married first. But by the family's New Year's Eve reunion, will all three have learned what it means to be really lucky—in love?

Nicholas Cole-Thomas is the ultimate eligible bachelor. But when beautiful veterinarian Peyton Blackstone needs help, he invites her to stay on his horse farm. And the closer he gets to her, the closer he wants to be….

"Smoking-hot love scenes, a fascinating story and extremely likable characters combine in a thrilling book that's hard to put down." —*RT Book Reviews* on *Sweet Dreams*